Dear Team
Hope you enjoy this!
All the best
Mei

ALL ANGELS HAVE WINGS

Mai Thomsen

authorHOUSE®

AuthorHouse™ UK
1663 Liberty Drive
Bloomington, IN 47403 USA
www.authorhouse.co.uk
Phone: UK TFN: 0800 0148641 (Toll Free inside the UK)
UK Local: (02) 0369 56322 (+44 20 3695 6322 from outside the UK)

© 2022 Mai Thomsen. All rights reserved.

No part of this book may be reproduced, stored in a retrieval system, or transmitted by any means without the written permission of the author.

This is a work of fiction. All of the characters, names, incidents, organizations, and dialogue in this novel are either the products of the author's imagination or are used fictitiously.

Published by AuthorHouse 11/21/2022

ISBN: 978-1-7283-7640-0 (sc)
ISBN: 978-1-7283-7641-7 (hc)
ISBN: 978-1-7283-7639-4 (e)

Print information available on the last page.

Any people depicted in stock imagery provided by Getty Images are models, and such images are being used for illustrative purposes only.
Certain stock imagery © Getty Images.

This book is printed on acid-free paper.

Because of the dynamic nature of the Internet, any web addresses or links contained in this book may have changed since publication and may no longer be valid. The views expressed in this work are solely those of the author and do not necessarily reflect the views of the publisher, and the publisher hereby disclaims any responsibility for them.

THANK YOU NOTE

If I have learned anything from my life it is that you decide what family means to you, and when people feel like sunlight, stay in that sunlight, and don't retract back to the shadows.

Thank you to my sunlight – to the people supporting me through this journey, and to my schoolteacher for inspiring me to start writing all those years ago. This would not have been possible without you all.

PROLOGUE

The sound of the shovel was deafening, and he was in no hurry. Took one slow but determined dig, one after the other. The soil slowly building in a pile next to him while the hole in the ground now reached his knees. At no point in time did he puff or complain, almost like he did not tire. He just kept digging and whistling the same short melody over and over.

"Fffff fff fff fff, ff-fff fff fffff fff ff-fff." Trish didn't recognise the tune, but she knew that his whistling, along with sounds of the soil brushing against the shovel, would be the last things she heard. She was going to die. She could already feel it. The stab wound was bad, and she had been bleeding for hours now, going in and out of consciousness. She just hoped it would all end before she was put in the ground. Before the soil suffocated her and the ground took claim over her body.

She thought about her family. Imagined that it was just a regular Sunday. They would all have breakfast together before going to the park, and Darren would play rugby with the boys and later complain about his sore back and aching muscles. Their two sons were getting big. Eleven and sixteen. How time had passed so quickly was still a mystery to her. It felt just like yesterday that her youngest had taken his first steps while his older brother had started school. Back then, Sunday playtime in the park had been a lot different. Now the boys were all grown up, and they gave their dad a run for his money. Darren would not admit it, but the boys getting bigger and stronger might not have been the only factor in why they were now beating him. With them growing up, each day he too was getting older.

Trish smiled and ignored the throbbing pain from her stomach. She was not ready to leave this memory yet and held her eyes tightly closed and returned as Darren was walking towards her with a smile on his face.

She and Darren had met later in life, and their love had been instant. They had both been married at the time. Both married young, so it had caused quite the scandal, but their love had been immediate, the kind you only read about in books and watched in movies. Neither of them had kids at the time; it was not something they had ever wanted or even talked about, but when the test came back positive, they had been overjoyed. Their son, Jason, had been a surprise of the best kind, and it had just felt right. They had not planned on having any more kids, so just like the first time around, it had completely caught them by surprise when the test was positive again. Their second son, Liam, had not just been a great surprise; he had also been the missing piece to their hearts. When he arrived, it was like their family was completed, like they had been waiting for him all along.

She smiled and took a breath, felt her husband wrap a blanket around her shoulders. She felt lighter, like he was telling her to let go, that they would be okay. They would be sad and confused, but they were strong individuals, and they had each other to lean on. She was certain that they would be okay. *They will be okay*, she thought to herself again. Even if she was no longer with them. The whole family was there to protect them. Grandparents, their father, uncles, and aunties. *They will be okay*, she thought again.

She was ready. Took another deep breath and tried to let go. Death could take her now; it was alright.

The shovelling stopped; so did the whistling. All that was left was the sounds of the empty forest.

He started moving again. She could hear the nettles under his boots. He sat down beside her and touched her cheek, wiping away some tears she hadn't noticed falling.

"I am sorry, Trish," he whispered. "But you are not the angel I was looking for."

She met his eyes. She didn't want to, but she was drawn to them. He had such beautiful eyes. The moon provided enough light for her to see the outline of his face. He was quite handsome, beautiful even. Light blue eyes and a sharp jaw. He was just in a t-shirt and didn't seem to bother with the cold temperatures or the rain gently falling around them. The rain made the shirt hug his body, made it seem like the shirt was made for his body, and the muscles were not just for show. He lifted her up like nothing; she almost felt weightless. Laid her back down on the cold ground in the hole he had just made.

"I am sorry," he said again, stroking her cheek once more and removing a few strains of hair from her face before resting his palm on her neck. His hand was warm. "You are beautiful; I shouldn't have lost control like that. You just made me upset when you tried to run away. I was not going to hurt you, not really." He leaned in close, his cheek meeting hers sending shivers through her body. "I was just wanting to give you wings." He smiled. "Make you an angel." His smile grew wider as he gently moved his hand down over her body. "My angel," he said just above a whisper, his eyes turning black with arousal. He was shaking as his hand came to a halt, and he leaned in again. Licked her cheek. "For you see …" He turned her face so she could see his eyes. "… all angels have wings."

She was trembling under his touch and hoped death would come quickly as her eyes met his. The soft blue eyes from before were now cold and dark, and his handsome features were almost inhuman. Even his blond hair looked dark now, and she had a feeling she had met the devil himself.

He tried to kiss her, and she flinched, causing a wide smile on his face. He stood up and lifted himself with ease from the hole in the ground. Then he picked up the shovel and slowly started moving the soil. Trish felt a new pain, a heavy pain in her chest. *I am going to die now*, she thought. *I am going to be buried alive.*

The soil was covering her legs, and she felt it hard to move. Her hands were still tied, and she could see the soil slowly falling onto her stomach. He was taking his time, had started whistling again, and her hopes of dying from the stab wound seemed to vanish. She could hardly even feel it anymore. Losing consciousness was also not an option, as her body was panicking and pumping with adrenalin. The longer he took, the more her stupid mind started hoping he would stop, change his mind. That this was all a scare game to warn her from trying to run away again. She wanted to tell him she understood, she wasn't going to try anything else, but she couldn't speak. Her voice had gone, and she knew it would take a miracle for her to get out of this.

She closed her eyes, tried to find the memory of her family once more.

The soil had reached her neck, and small pieces were rolling onto her face, grazing her chin and then falling onto the ground beside her head.

She was back in the park with her husband and kids, watching them as they played and laughed in front of her. She was about to call them over for lunch, when a familiar sound made her eyes shoot open. She didn't recognise it at first, but it brought a strong sense of hope through her. *Sirens*, she thought. There were sirens in the distance.

He must have heard them too. The soil had stopped falling, and he stood still in his tracks. Every muscle in his body tensed as he listened. The sirens did not disappear; they came closer, slowly closing the distance to them. Had they realised that she was missing? Did they know where he was taking them? How did they know, how could they know? The thoughts ran through his mind in matter of seconds. His grip around the shovel tightened.

"No," he hissed. He wasn't done, not yet. He still hadn't found his angel. "No." He winced again and almost broke the shovel with his bare hands.

Trish started moving again, fighting the soil that he was now forcefully throwing on top of her. She could taste it, feel it in her nose and throat. She wanted to cough or turn her head, but opening her mouth invited more soil in. It was a losing game, and the sirens had disappeared. She couldn't hear them anymore. They were not going to arrive in time. She wasn't going to make it.

Soil was covering her face now as her head kept moving, kept searching for that millimetre of free space for her to breathe. She was holding her breath, fighting to get to air, but eventually she had to open her mouth. She had to. Her mouth filled with soil, and she tried to cough but couldn't. The soil on top of her was getting heavy, and there was no longer any air left to breathe in.

The sirens had changed direction and then died out. It made him growl and toss the shovel to the ground. He had gotten distracted by them, had hurried, and not taken his time. He had not even seen her face as it had been covered. He had been too occupied with getting the job done. Everything about this woman had been a disaster. She had been much older than the rest of them and a lot stronger. She had really put up a fight.

He hadn't meant to take her. It had only been a few days since the last one, but her smile had distracted him. Her smile had been just like his angels. Just like it. He knew it could not have been her, the age was all wrong, but she just looked so much like her. So much.

He cracked his neck and took a deep breath. It was done now. She was gone, and everything was back on track. *No more distractions*, he thought as he stomped on the ground. The small patches of grass were skilfully placed back, and he tossed some sticks and leaves on the ground, making the grave invisible.

"No more," he repeated and looked around.

The ground looked just like any other forest. Trees and bushes grew close and entangled with the thick moss and grass. It looked untouched, virgin almost, like a hidden secret deep within the woods. His secret, his paradise. And only he knew what was hidden underneath it all.

He bent down on his knees and unbuckled his belt. So many failed projects, so many lives lost. So many. But none of them had wings, none of them had been able to fly like her. There was only one true angel, only one who could fly.

"It is time, my angel," he whispered and smiled, feeling the arousal build. She was out there; she had to be. He just knew it. "I am coming, my angel." He closed his eyes and remembered her smile and her gentle hands. "I am coming to find you. And I want you to know I am coming."

He gathered his things from the forest ground and placed a little white rock in between the sticks and leaves where Trish had been buried. A camera clicked, and the flash lit up the ground for a split-second.

"Goodbye, Trish," he whispered before he made his way through the woods, bag and shovel in hand and a smile plastered on his face.

He moved smoothly and disappeared in the dark, all the while his whistling was echoing through the trees. "Fffff fff fff fff, ff-fff fff fffff fff ff-fff."

CHAPTER 1

Linda parked the car and just sat there for a while, tightly gripping the steering wheel as she watched the crowd slowly making their way into the church. She put the key back in the ignition and thought for a second about just starting it back up and driving away. She doubted anyone in there would miss her. They would almost certainly assume that she wouldn't show up, anyway. Their expectations for her had never been very high. She had always been the black sheep of the family—the disappointment no one really talked about.

She drew in a shaky breath, folded her arms over the wheel, and rested her forehead against them. *I am okay. It is going to be okay. I am okay. I am okay.*

"One, two, three, four, five." She kept her eyes shut as she counted and tried to focus on her breathing. "Six, seven, eight, nine, ten." Her chest was raising rapidly, and her breaths were getting shorter. *Keep it together, Hemmer. Keep it together.* "Eleven, twelve, thirteen, fourteen, fifteen." She counted slower, started tapping her foot in a slow rhythm. *You are okay. Just keep breathing. Keep breathing.*

"I need to you keep breathing for me, love. Can you do that?"

Linda felt the world spinning as they walked up to the church. The hand in hers tightened its grip, and she could feel a second hand against her chest.

"It is just me, love. It's just me."

Warm breath hit her cheek, and she felt herself wrapped in a tight hug.

"I got you. I promise."

Linda felt tears on her shoulder, and the arms around her started shaking.

"I need you to come back to me, please. I can't do this by myself. I need you, Linda, please."

Linda took a few deep breaths and then wrapped her arms around the woman holding her. "I am here," Linda whispered back. Her voice cracked, and her hands were still trembling. "I am here. I am okay. We are okay."

The grip around her loosened, and a pair of teary green eyes met hers. "I am sorry," Linda whispered as she lowered her face and looked at the ground, tears now streaming down her cheeks.

"It is not your fault, love. It isn't." She felt a pair of hands on her cheeks wiping away the tears. "Hey, look at me. Linda, please look at me." A hand gently lifted her chin, and she felt a brief kiss on her lips. "It is not your fault, okay? I need to hear you say it. Please say it with me: It is not your fault."

"It is not my fault," Linda repeated and nodded before she embraced the woman again in a tight hug and buried her face in the crook of her neck. "It is not my fault," she cried and felt calming strokes down her back.

"Come, love. We should get inside."

They held each other's hands tightly again and shared a look. "Our little girl needs us one last time, okay? So we have to do this."

Linda nodded and walked alongside her wife into the church and up the aisle. Everyone looked at them, but Linda she didn't notice. Her eyes were solely fixed on the little coffin at the end and the framed photo on top. Willa looked so happy in that photo. She was smiling from ear to ear and proudly showing off the ladybug she had on her nose. Linda stifled a laugh at the memory and sat down on the bench, waiting for the service to begin.

"It is okay," she said as her wife broke down crying. "You are okay; just keep breathing."

Just keep breathing. "Sixteen, seventeen, eighteen, nineteen, twenty."

She raised her head from the steering wheel and slowly opened her eyes. Her breathing had slowed, and the pain in her chest had gone. She had been crying this whole time. Never in her life had she thought herself able to cry so much.

She took another look up at the church. She couldn't attend another funeral, lose more of her family. Maybe it was better if she just stayed away. *Maybe they don't even want me there,* she thought, but she quickly pushed it away as she thought of her grandmother. *Gran would have wanted me there.*

It had come as a shock to everyone when their gran had passed. Sure, she was not getting any younger, and many would say she had lived far longer than most, but she had just always been such a survivor, a true inspiration.

Before Gran was born, both of her parents had tried fleeing north, escaping the war in their country, but her father had been captured and killed, while her mother had died in child labour, and she herself had been handed off to an orphanage, where she had stayed till the age of sixteen. At seventeen, she had married, and by twenty-one, she had had three children.

By twenty-four, her husband had passed in an accident, and she had been left to raise their children on her own. Thankfully, he had been a wealthy man, and after selling their house, she and her children continued to live a good life. By twenty-seven, she had fallen in love and remarried, and, shortly after, two more children joined the family.

Then a tragedy hit. She fell off a horse in an accident and was deemed paralysed from the waist down, never to walk again. But she had proven them all wrong, and after years and years of medical treatments and physiotherapy, she was back on her feet. A miracle, doctors had said. From then she had always walked tall and refused to let it show that she had once been crippled.

Years passed, and the children grew up. Modern times had come, and she and her husband had started travelling the world. They settled down in Italy for a while before returning home when their first grandchild had arrived. She had been the best grandmother in the world—and, in time, also the best great-grandmother. She was the glue holding the whole family together. So when she got diagnosed with breast cancer, it had sent a shock through them all. No one could imagine a life without her in it. Thankfully, she was strong as an ox, and what was a little breast cancer to a woman who had survived so much already?

A few years later, she lost her husband to pancreatic cancer, and that seemed to have been her biggest defeat in life. Her heart was broken from the loss, but she never once let it show. She always stayed bright and optimistic, and continued to encourage joy and laughter in everyone's life.

No one had ever imagined that a simple cold would have gotten the better of her.

A true inspiration, Linda repeated in her head and smiled at the memory of her grandmother.

She took a couple of deep breaths and finally made her way towards the church.

"Mom, it's hot in here, and this tie is itchy," Jason complained quietly.

"And I have to pee," Liam countered. Trish sighed and turned to her husband. Darren just gave her a reassuring look and kissed her before signalling for the boys to follow him out of the church.

"Are you okay?" Helen asked as she sat down beside her older sister. Trish nodded briefly and took her hand. Today was going to be a rough day for them all.

"Do you think she is coming?" Helen didn't have to specify who she was referring to. There was only one person missing, and Trish doubted very much that she would have the decency to show up.

"Nah, why would she? Not like she has ever been there for her family. Why should she start now?" Trish answered with a coldness to her voice, while she seemed to tighten the grip around her big sister's hand.

"Bit harsh there, Trish," Paul protested as he sat down with his older sisters.

"Well, the truth hurts," Trish mumbled and thought how, of course, Paul would take their little sister's side. He had always been so protective of her. Paul just took a deep breath and almost hoped that the youngest of the four would not show up. He just wanted them to get through this one day without fighting. Their mother seemed to think the same, as she passed them down the aisle and gave them a stern look.

"Behave," she said firmly as she made her way to the front row to sit beside her husband. "This is your grandmother's funeral. She wouldn't want you to fight."

Trish was about to rise from her seat when Helen stopped her.

"Not today," she said simply as the church bells started tolling, indicating the service was about to start.

"Are you kidding me?" Trish protested through her teeth. "We are not fighting." She lowered her voice and looked around. "Besides, Gran would love it. She would walk around taking bets on who would win."

They had to agree with her on that, all three of them smiling at the thought of it.

"And I think we all know how bad your odds would have been." A familiar voice cut through, and the three siblings turned their heads to the aisle and were met by a set of familiar bright-blue eyes.

"You made it," Helen said a little too loud for a church setting. But she didn't care. She just took her beloved sister in for a warm embrace. "We didn't think you would make it back in time."

Linda smiled and hugged her back, only just now realising how much she had missed her family. A tear rolled down her cheek as Helen released her grip, and she felt Paul's strong arms around her next. She rested her cheek against his chest. Nothing ever felt safer than standing there with her big brother's arms wrapped tightly around her.

"We missed you," he whispered and gave her a final squeeze before they were interrupted by their parents.

"Oh, Linda honey," their mom cried out as she held her daughter tightly.

"About time you showed up," her father's voice interrupted, and Linda avoided his gaze. They exchanged a few words and looks before they all returned to their seats, and the service began.

It wasn't until then, they realised that in their hurry to find their seats, they had placed Trish and Linda next to each other. Paul and Helen exchanged a look, and Paul considered getting up and sitting between the two, but then the music started playing and the choir director turned to start the initial prayers. *God be with us*, he thought to himself and eyed his sisters, as they also seemed to have realised now how close they were in proximity.

Paul caught Helen's eye, and they seemed to have the same thought: *This was it.* Chaos would erupt any second now. Their sisters were undoubtedly going to make a scene and cause havoc as always, and Gran would sit in heaven with popcorn and enjoy it like it was an MMA fight. They waited and waited, but disaster never strook, and they thought maybe their sisters would act grown up for once.

"You can shed tears that she is gone, or you can smile because she has lived," the priest said. "You can close your eyes and pray that she will come back, or you can open your eyes and see all that she has left. Your heart can be empty because you can't see her, or you can be full of the love that you shared. You can turn your back on tomorrow and live yesterday, or you can be happy for tomorrow because of yesterday. You can remember her and only that she is gone, or you can cherish her memory and let it live on. You can cry and close your mind, be empty and turn your back, or you can do what she would want: smile, open your eyes, love, and go on."

"David Harkins," Trish and Linda whispered simultaneously and exchanged a look. They both had blank and red-streaked eyes, and both smiled as they remembered their grandmother's fondness of the English poet.

Trish blinked and snapped her head back at the priest. She trembled as tears fell over her cheeks and her hands started shaking. Linda didn't think twice before wrapping an arm around her older sister, drawing her in.

"I am glad you made it," Trish whispered and leaned into the embrace.

"Me too." Linda smiled and rested her head against her shoulder. "Me too."

They finished the last song, and a soft melody started playing.

Paul got up along with their father and cousins, and together they carried Gran's coffin to the car before her final resting place.

The three sisters, Trish, Helen, and Linda got up together and followed the crowd out of the church, never once loosening the tight grip they had on each other. Paul joined them as they followed the car, and all joined around the grave.

"It will be okay," Linda whispered as she felt Trish shake by her side. "We have each other. Whatever else happens, we will always have each other." She tightened her grip further around her sister's shoulders.

"Promise?" Trish asked quietly through her tears and suddenly felt herself the younger one of the two. She sighed as she felt all three of her siblings close in around her.

"Yes, I promise," Linda reassured her.

CHAPTER 2

Loved ones started moving about and returning back to their cars. They were supposed to meet up at Gran's house for the post-service courtesies. Paul and Helen left with their respective partners and kids, while Trish let her husband and kids drive ahead without her. She herself stayed behind a bit longer with Linda before they too drove to the house. They were quiet on the ride, still getting used to being this close to each other again.

When Linda switched off the car but didn't take the keys out of the ignition, Trish realised that nothing had changed.

"You are not coming in, are you?" It wasn't really a question.

"I am sorry, Trish, but I have to go back."

"Why?"

"Work," Linda answered simply. It wasn't a lie, but she knew it wasn't what her sister wanted to hear.

"I miss you," Trish stated. "So much has happened, and we have so much to talk about. I just, I just really miss my little sister."

Trish looked broken, and Linda wanted to say that she would stay; she wished she didn't have to go back, but she did. She had to. Her job was not finished yet. They had even bent the rules, if not broken them, just allowing her to attend this funeral. "Stay," Trish pleaded. "If not for me, then for the kids. They miss their cool aunt."

Linda smiled at that. Being an aunt to those kids was truly the best thing.

Trish had been the first one of them to have kids, though she got them late. A real scandal in the little town when she and Darren first had gotten together. Linda remembered that time well, because for once, she had not been the talk of the town. Her and Darren had met, and it had been like fireworks. He had filed for divorce from his high school sweetheart, while

Trish had divorced the town's wealthiest man, whom she had just recently married.

The scandal had gotten even better when their brother Paul announced his engagement to a student who was ten years his junior; she was pregnant within the first year. Though the icing on the cake had been when their sister Helen had come home from her year-long trip to Nigeria as a volunteer health worker and introduced everyone to her boyfriend, Lincoln. It had been a shock that she had finally found someone, but what really stood out was his skin colour, in a town of white supremacists.

Their parents had never viewed themselves as racist, and maybe they were right in that, but they were also not actively *not* racist, something that became very clear to them the more time they spent with Lincoln. It was still not perfect, but they were trying, and Lincoln was a patient man, willing to take the time to educate them.

If only they had shown the same willingness to listen and learn when Linda had introduced them to her first girlfriend. Her mother had since warmed to the idea and even attended her wedding, whereas her father was still in denial. They hadn't had a proper conversation in almost eighteen years.

"You should go inside." Linda's voice broke the silence. "They are all waiting."

"I really wish you would come with me," Trish begged one last time.

"I can't, not yet." Silence fell over them again, and they just sat there for a while longer, neither wanting to make a move to leave the other. "I love you, you know." Linda spoke suddenly, and Trish started cackling.

"Gosh, that was weird." She laughed, and Linda joined in.

"It was, wasn't it?" Linda agreed. "I guess we don't say that a lot in our family. Felt weird." They fell quiet again, and Trish took her hand.

"I love you too, little sis." This time, it was Linda's turn shrug and laugh it off.

"You are right, that is weird. God, we are a weird family."

"Nah, I think we are pretty normal. But speaking of love, have you spoken with Andrea, since coming back?" Trish shoved her sister playfully with her elbow. Linda made a face and shook her head. "Why not? Is there someone else?"

"Trish," Linda warned.

"What? I am your big sister; I'm supposed to know about these things. Even if we are not teenagers anymore and not sitting braiding each other's hair on Gran's bed or fighting over her jewellery. I still want to know what is going on in your life. Even if we are fighting, I want to know." Her voice went more serious. "I need to know you are okay."

Linda sighed and squeezed her hand before she turned to her and spoke.

"First off, you and I were never teenagers at the same time; you were all grown up and out of the house by the time I got out of diapers. And secondly, I would never play with jewellery or braid anyone's hair; I played with fire trucks and magic cards." Trish laughed.

"Yeah, you were a strange kid. Thinking back, it really shouldn't have come as a surprise when you told us you were gay."

"I don't think trucks and magic cards had anything to do with it," Linda said and laughed quietly.

"Probably not." Tish went quiet again before she turned in her seat and looked at her sister. "Just, please tell me you will be safe? That, you—that you will come home?" Her eyes were blank, and Linda could tell she was holding back tears. There had been enough pain today, and she just wanted to reassure her.

"I promise. I will be safe. I will come home." The lies spilled so easily over her lips, so easy Linda almost believed them herself.

"You better. If not, I am going to find a way to resurrect you and kill you myself." There was humour in her statement, but she meant it, and there was nothing funny about it.

Trish finally made her way into the house and watched as her sister drove away, leaving the family behind yet again. She never understood why Linda took that job or why she enrolled in the army in the first place, let alone working for the police. But then again, she had never really been able to comprehend what Linda had gone through. None of them had. They only ever heard what the police had told them and what the news outlets conspired about. Linda never once spoke about it. And they never asked. Trish had been abroad in Australia at the time and had never really gotten the full picture of what had happened. As Linda had said, Trish was almost already moved out of the house by the time Linda was born.

Trish had promised herself to ask her sister, but when she returned home, no one wanted to talk about it, and Linda had gone away for treatment.

Then later in life, the tragedy with little Willa happened, and Linda just closed herself off from the world, buried herself in work and put her life on hold. Trish kept telling herself that if she just knew the truth, then she would understand Linda's decision. Maybe even be at peace with it, but part of her doubted she would accept her choice, even if she knew the reason why. Mostly because she herself could never in a million years imagine leaving her family behind.

"Heeey, Mom! There you are. We were beginning to wonder if the two of you had made it to the car or if you were fighting it off amongst the tombstones," Jason joked, and Trish gave her sixteen-year-old a stern look. "Oh, come on, Mom, that was funny."

"Mom," Liam shouted. "Did Aunty kick your ass?" He received a high-five from his older brother.

"Liam," Trish exclaimed, looking from one son to the other. "Is it your father teaching you this kind of language?" She searched the room for her husband.

"Don't blame me," Darren said and held up his hands. "I am not the one fighting my siblings on holy ground." He teased her, and their boys tried to hide their wide grins. *Of course, he would take their side.* Trish shook her head and went looking for the bar. *There had to be alcohol hidden somewhere, right?*

She greeted people quietly, as she made her way through the house and sighed in relief when she saw a beautiful man standing in the piano room behind the bar. He was mixing a cocktail, and Trish hoped he had something stronger than a whiskey sour.

"Hello, miss, what can I get you?" he asked while shaking the mixer like he was trying to turn milk into butter.

"Do you have tequila?" she asked, and he flashed her a smile.

"Say no more." He finished making the cocktail before pouring two shots. "To the ones we loved and lost," he said, and they emptied their drinks in one go.

"Thank you." Trish smiled. "I really needed that."

She placed the glass back on the counter and asked for a refill before checking her phone. She thought about calling Linda, explaining the real reason why she was upset with her. Why everything had gone to shit, and why she had blamed her for so long. But she wasn't ready to have that conversation; she wasn't ready for her sister to hate her all over again. *Maybe when she comes home again,* she thought to herself and was about to empty the glass a second time, when she saw it was still empty. She looked up and was met with a wondering look from the handsome man at the bar. His eyes seemed glued to her, which got her to unconsciously touch the frames of her glasses.

"Sorry, do I have something on my face?" she asked.

That seemed to shake him out of whatever he was thinking, and he forced a smile.

"No, no, sorry; y-you just remind of someone I used to know." He seemed nervous all of a sudden, and Trish instinctively reached for his hand with a gentle touch.

"Are you okay?" she asked with a slight smile.

The man seemed frazzled but shook it off.

"I'm pretty sure I am supposed to ask you that," he joked and poured them another shot.

"Yeah, well, I am all about caring for everyone else these days," Trish said and emptied the glass again.

She didn't say anything else, just made her way to the piano and sat down. Her first touch on the keys was a bit shaky, but once she started playing, it was like she had never done anything else.

Quickly, the family gathered around her and started singing along.

What a wonderful voice, the bartender thought and touched his hand where she had rested hers. *Gentle touch and a beautiful smile.* He moved in the crowd till he caught sight of the woman at the piano.

"My angel," he whispered and felt himself smirk.

CHAPTER 3

The rich forest smell of fire and dry wood seeped through the living room, in battle with scented candles and Mrs. Buch's homemade potpourri. Streaks of silver smoke curled and danced through the house, excited to escape the gentle pull from the chimney. Flames leaped behind the barrier of the fireplace, and the heat spread to all the nooks and crannies.

Arnold Buch sat in his favourite chair with his feet firmly planted on the stool in front of the fire and a pipe hanging from the corner of his mouth. These were the moments he enjoyed and appreciated the most. Some peace and quiet while meditating in his chair. *Meditating,* he chuckled to himself. His wife would laugh out loud at that. Probably pointing out that he needed to work on his breathing, since it came out as more of a snore. He continued to chuckle as he sighed and relaxed in his chair.

Tomorrow, it would all change. The Christmas holidays started, and the house would be filled. It was the first Christmas in years where they would all be together. After the kids had moved away from home, they had joined them for Christmas on a rotational basis, but this time, they would all be there together.

They had three children together, him and Annelise. Daniel was the oldest. He worked as a graphic designer, and along with Joyce, his architect wife, they had been making plans for building their dream home. Arnold had found it outrageous to spend that much money on a house, but his son wouldn't budge, and good the same. Now they had the most wonderful home, and as a father, Arnold could not have been prouder. Well, maybe if his son would deliver him some grandkids, but Daniel and Joyce did not seem to be wanting children anytime soon.

After Daniel were the twins, Margret and Elisa. Much like their older brother, they too had focused on their careers and made great lives for themselves.

Margret was a marine biologist and had travelled the world to discover plant life and save those endangered from extinction. It was on one of her trips that she had met Brandon, and for many years, they had thrown their love into saving flowers. Nonsense, if you asked Arnold, but he knew his daughter well enough not to start an argument. She was much too like her mother this one. Hot-headed and stubborn, and he knew he didn't stand a chance against her.

Her twin, Elisa, was just the same. Two pieces cut from the same cloth. He smiled, thinking back on the grey hairs they had caused him in their teens. Sneaking out at night and keeping secrets. Now they both had kids of their own, and let's just say, karma is real.

Margret and Brandon had two boys, aged one and three, and they were expecting their third child come summertime. Elisa was also pregnant. She and her husband, Thomas, were expecting twins early in the new year, and with Thomas's seven-year-old son from a previous relationship, they too had their hands full.

They all grew up so fast, and Arnold had a hard time keeping up. He remembered it as just a few years ago, they were all small and ran around his legs. The girls had adored their father and always waited patiently for him to come home from work. Looking back, Arnold wished he could have spent more time with them instead of working. But he had been and would always be a workaholic. Gratefully, his relationship with his daughters had remained, and they still looked up to him and asked for his advice.

It was much the same with Daniel. As a kid, he had followed his father around and copied his every move. Arnold had referred to him as his mini self, and he had been certain that Daniel would have followed in his footsteps and become a police officer. He had been so proud when his son had enlisted in the army, but it had quickly proven not to be David's cup of tea. He had been much too kind-hearted, and he had instead followed his passion into arts. It had been the right decision, and as a father, Arnold could respect that.

Three children and (for now) three grandchildren, and they all came home for Christmas. It had been a long time since they had all been gathered in one place, so this year, they had made a whole holiday out of it, and there were plenty of rooms in the big house.

Five minutes more, and his wife would get out of the bath.

He moved in the chair, and the pipe tilted in the corner of his mouth. He puffed it a few more times before he put it out and placed it in his pocket. His wife was not fond of tobacco smoke inside, but what could it hurt when the fireplace was lit, along with candles and scented sticks? He waved the newspaper in front of him and saw the smoke wipe out. Some remaining scents hung in the air, shining like ghosts in the breeze from the newspaper.

It was a matter of seconds now before his nap would be ruined, and he would be chased around here and there to get everything ready. It should be clean and tidy throughout the house. All the rooms had to be in order, the beds had to be made, and duvets and pillows had to be fetched from the loft.

It was the same stress and hustle every time someone came to stay, but after forty-two years of marriage, plus a few years of dating before then, he had become accustomed to it. They had their routine; his wife shouted at him with orders and tasks, and he did as she asked, even though he would much rather sit in his chair with his legs up and the pipe in his mouth.

He was always accused by his wife of not doing enough at home, and even though she was right, it was easiest not to break that pattern. That's how it had always been. He was very conservative in that area.

"I tell you, darling, if you do not get your butt lifted off that chair, I'll glue it to you," Annelise shouted through the house. *Not initially a bad solution*, Arnold thought to himself, smiling before pulling the small handle on the side of the chair. The springs gave way and creaked as the backrest rose.

His body had left an imprint on the seat. The chair was old, and the imprint had become permanent. Had it been up to his wife, the chair would have been thrown out many years ago. But then he had set his foot down. If she wanted her orchids and a thousand little meaningless objects, then he could have his chair too. And despite recurring quarrels, it remained that way.

"Honey, your cell phone is ringing," his wife called again from the bathroom. "If it's Daniel, then you can tell him we do not have room for the dogs as well." She shouted through the sound from the hair dryer.

"It's from work," he shouted back, apologising in the phone to the office.

"You promised you wouldn't work this Christmas."

The hair dryer was switched off, and Annelise appeared in the hallway. Her eyes said everything. She did not stand there long. A few seconds of eye contact was enough for her to make her opinion clear. Arnold exhaled heavily and turned around. Asked the office if it was important or if he could call back later.

"My wife will not appreciate this," he started. "Are you aware that you are putting a marriage on the line just by calling?" He was greeted with laughter on the phone from his partner.

Iversen, at thirty-five years of age still young, had not yet found love, and from his many conquest stories, it did not sound as if it would happen anytime soon. He was a rookie in many areas, so Arnold gave up in explaining the rules of marriage. There was still so much the young man did not yet understand.

Iversen had a natural talent for crimes and homicides, and was born to be in law enforcement. He had a way to think ahead of the killer, like he could read their minds. The only flaw of this young man in the field of investigation was that he was quick to form a theory, and he often let his first impressions cloud his judgement. First impressions were essential in an investigation, but the young officer had it in him to let his prejudices overshadow everything else, so he still had lots to learn, and Arnold had sought out to teach him.

Iversen's knowledge extended far and wide, and when it came to electronics, it was suddenly Arnold who was the rookie and had to learn from the younger generation. There was no doubt that Iversen's head was screwed on properly. He just needed the last training to become a great investigator, and it was Arnold's virtue and honour to train him.

Annelise came out of the bathroom and spun around with a big smile. She had bought a new dress for Christmas and wanted to try it on before tomorrow. The red fabric swung around her as she rotated. Her nails and lips were painted in the same deep red colour, and her long light brown hair was straightened and danced around her shoulders, grey streaks breaking the colour in a natural way.

"Arnold," she exclaimed, disappointed, stopping in her rotation. Arnold raised his hand dismissively and returned to his conversation.

It was the same every time. Work always came first. Forty-something years together, and she kept trying to change him. She could not afford to be angry with him, because she knew him. He was and would always be a perfectionistic workaholic; even age could not change that.

She both rejoiced and dreaded the day he would retire. It should be great to have him at home and maybe see him lend a helping hand every now and then. Though, she did not have high expectations in that area. But what would become of him when he did not have his job? If he could no longer solve murders and crimes, how would he pass time? *What will become of my Arnold?*

Several times throughout the years, she had considered divorcing him, but in the end, she couldn't. Because even though he was self-absorbed and focused on his job, he was the same honest, sensitive, and warm-hearted man she had fallen in love with.

From the very first moment, he had managed to sweep her off her feet, and he held her heart forever. She still remembered it as if it were yesterday when he had been walking on the road, and she had spotted him in the side-mirror. At that time, he had been a newly trained police officer and had looked extremely handsome and sexy in his uniform, which he had worn with pride every day since.

It had not been her intention to flirt with him at first, but at the sight of his figure in the mirror, he had her swooning. She had given her breasts a slight push towards the chin, while a couple of shirt buttons had been opened and the skirt pulled up above her knees. She had even managed to straighten her hair and fix her lipstick before Officer Arnold Buch had knocked on her window.

The encounter with his dark eyes had made the final impact, and she had been magnetised on the spot. He, too, had been dazed after the meeting, and only after waving goodbye to her had he discovered the note with the fine in his hand. Her beauty had blown him away and he had completely forgotten what he was doing.

He was, of course, good at his job even then, and as the good officer he was, he took the time to seek her out and hand her the fine, after which she invited him inside for coffee. The rest was history.

She shook her head at the memory and disappeared into the living room. Arnold saw her out of the corner of his eye and knew he had failed. Even a crime commissioner who was used to being respected and at times feared at work could spin like a cat and walk on tiptoes at home. Terrible criminals and murderers were nothing compared to the killing gaze of a wife.

Arnold knew that a trip to the office would boost a new quarrel, and he could not bear that before the children and grandchildren came home. *I guess it is also time for Iversen to oversee his own investigation?* He wasn't exactly alone in that thought. Arnold had done a lot to teach the younger man that police work was not like on TV. No one handled the cases on their own. It was collaboration that made the difference, and Iversen was in safe hands with the team. Maybe Arnold should just throw him into it?

"Is it really necessary for me to come in?" he asked.

"Yes," agreed Jensen, who had come to the phone.

He and Arnold were old friends and had worked on many cases together. If he said it was serious, then there was nothing else to do. Arnold had to go to the office.

"We need you on this one," Jensen repeated, as if to put pressure on the necessity of Arnold being present. Arnold took a deep breath as he prepared to explain it all to Annelise.

He waited a little while out in the hallway and came subtly towards his wife, like a pig ready for slaughter. She stood at the dining table, putting the finishing touches on the table setting.

"You are going into the office, aren't you?" she asked.

"I guess I have to," he replied cautiously.

"Yes," she said quietly. "I had no doubt once I saw the news." She pointed in the direction of the television. It was muted, and yet the screams and cries of the families cut through to the bone.

A large crowd of people had gathered on the field just outside the old forest. Blue lights blinked, and police officers tried to keep people back. A few journalists had gotten through barrier and were broadcasting between the trees. The sight made Arnold shiver. White upon white sheets covered bodies and graves. He started counting but quickly gave up once the frame widened, and more bodies came into sight.

"It is a gravesite," he whispered.

Annelise, too, was shaken, and Arnold put a reassuring arm around her, trying to find some comfort in that himself.

CHAPTER 4

Arnold stepped into the station with determination and still a scared look on his face from what he had just witnessed on the news. His hands were shaking as he opened the door, hoping to find Iversen at his desk, but the room was empty, and he was left to his own thoughts while waiting.

"Iversen," he called out, and quick steps sounded from the hallway. A tall man with blond hair and blue eyes hurried down the hall and seemed relieved when he saw Arnold.

"Thank you for coming in," Iversen said. "This one seems way out of my league." He dropped a stack of papers on the desk. His white face looked paler than usual, and Arnold guessed he had been there on the scene. An image like that would forever haunt one's dreams.

"Are you okay?" Arnold asked, resting a comforting hand on the younger man's shoulders.

"Yes, no. I don't know. Buch, it was terrible. There were so many bodies, so many. It was just, terrible. Just terrible."

Arnold hummed in agreement, and they stood still for bit. A comfortable silence filled the room.

"I am okay, Buch," Iversen finally said. "I promise."

Arnold nodded and took another look at his partner. He had gotten a bit of colour back in his face, and his shoulders dropped a little, though he still stood tall. Arnold couldn't help but compare the young man's figure to his own. They wore similar outfits, but Iversen's seemed to fit into his just right, a little tight around the shoulders. Arnold chuckled to himself. It was many years ago since his shirt had been too tight around the shoulders; now there were other areas where the fabric would no longer reach.

What I wouldn't give to be in my thirties again, he thought.

"There you are, Buch." A familiar voice cut through the silence as Jensen stepped through the door. He gave a movement with his head, and Iversen took the hint and left the room, closing the door behind him.

"You have a worried expression, my friend," Arnold began, and Jensen took a seat in front of him. The seriousness of the case was already clear before he began to explain.

Officers had spent most of the afternoon and evening counting bodies and preparing them for transport to the morgue.

"Thirty-two." It came out as a whisper, and Jensen's hands trembled as he started opening the first file.

"Anyone identified?"

"Not yet, but we seem to have the first names of everyone." Arnold's brows furrowed, and Jensen continued to explain. "Whoever buried them left little white stones scattered on the ground." He pulled a photo from the file. "Each stone belongs to a grave, and underneath each of them was written a name." He pulled a stack of photos out, each of them detailing the stones and the names written on them.

"Tombstones?" Arnold mumbled, and Jensen hummed.

"That is our assumption for now. Iversen and Rivers are pulling a list of missing people from the past twenty years."

"Twenty years? Do you really think these graves could be that old?"

"My guess is older. It is hard to say, only the top layer was soil, the rest was sand. So essentially, they were all buried in sand. Many of the bodies are very well preserved." Arnold felt his stomach turn and remembered one of his first cases. A husband had buried his wife on their private beach. Her body had not been discovered till many years later. Each day, the water had washed up on the beach and pushed the sand aside, till suddenly, her hand had been uncovered. So much of her body had still been intact, that it was hard to estimate a time of death. "This is a good thing for us," Jensen continued. "We have a lot more evidence with the bodies intact."

Silence fell over them again as they went through the photos. Thirty-two stones, thirty-two names, thirty-two lives lost. Taken before their time.

"They are all women." Arnold broke the silence, and Jensen nodded. "Thirty-two women missing. Why weren't we aware of this? I feel like this is something we should have seen coming."

"They could have been tourists. You know a lot of young kids come here on holiday. They could also be prostitutes, not a lot of them are reported missing."

"But still, they are human lives. Thirty-two is a lot of people."

Their talk was interrupted when Iversen came back with a list of names, everyone reported missing in the past twenty years.

"Is this for the whole country?" Arnold asked.

"Yes, most of it," Iversen replied. "We are still finding more. The other stations are filing in their reports. We should have the full list within a few days."

"We need them now," Jensen insisted, and Iversen made a noise.

"Sir, it is Christmas, not many people are working. It may take some time before we get the final names."

"Christmas," Jensen snorted. "Clearly, murderers don't celebrate Christmas." He started asking Iversen some questions. Arnold only listened with half an ear while he was still transfixed by the pictures from the scene.

He sorted them into two piles, one where the remains were mostly skeletons, and one where the whole body was intact. The pile with whole bodies was smaller than the other and therefore easier for him to concentrate on. Two of the women looked to have been killed very recently; they were all white and seemed to have brown hair, except for one, and in general all looked similar.

They were all naked, and their bodies were bruises. His mind went to a dark place, thinking of what they had gone through before ending up in the ground.

As he had daughters himself, he couldn't help but think that these young women were someone's daughters, sisters, wives, and maybe even mothers.

"This one looks older than the rest." He pointed to the only blonde woman in the mix. Iversen and Jensen turned to him and saw as he laid out the photos. "If you look at these ten, they look to be in their early twenties, maybe thirties. And then there is this one. She looks to be in her late forties at least, maybe even in her mid-fifties." He studied the pictures again and pointed out two photos. "These two, their bodies look new, fresh. I doubt they have been in the ground for more than a week."

"Mother and daughter maybe? Siblings?" Iversen suggested. "Or maybe he was targeting this one," pointing to the younger woman, "but then she surprised him, caught him, and he had to kill her too."

"Yeah, maybe."

"Huh," Jensen hummed and smiled slightly. "You could be right." He bummed the young man on his back. "Wise head on this one, eh, Buch?"

Arnold raised his head and nodded. "Yes, yes certainly." He wasn't quite sure what he agreed to, and he didn't care. "Can we go see the bodies?"

"Well, the morgue didn't have room for all of them, so we had to divide and conquer," Iversen explained, but Arnold was already on his feet.

"That's okay. I just want to see these two for now." He put the pictures of the two women on the whiteboard and made a circle around them. "These are the latest victims. This is where we start."

Loud heavy metal music was playing when they entered the morgue. *Dijana*, Arnold thought to himself with a soft smile. Good choice to have her on this case; she was the best. They knocked on the door, but no response came. Arnold carefully opened it and walked over to turn down the music.

"Jesus," Dijana exclaimed and jumped on the spot, wanting to throw something at them. "You scared the life out of me."

Iversen burst out laughing but quickly stopped himself, as no one else seemed to join in.

"What? That was funny," he tried. "I mean, we are in a morgue."

"We get it," Arnold snapped and then turned to address Dijana. "I am sorry we frightened you, but you must have known we would come by."

"Yeah, I guessed." She smiled and took off her gloves to greet them. "It is good to see you again, Buch. I just wish it was under different circumstances." He had to agree with her on that. "But I thought you were retiring."

"He is." Iversen answered for him and stepped forward, a wide smile plastered on his face. "Just two weeks left. I'm Jasper." He held his hand out and corrected himself, "Iversen. Sorry, I go by Iversen."

Dijana laughed to herself and shook his hand.

"Nice to meet you, Iversen," she said, and Iversen reminded himself to ask someone to kick him later for being stupid. He was usually great with women, never stumbled upon his words like now. *Circumstances*, he thought. *It had to be the circumstances.*

"Likewise." He smiled, trying to gain back his confidence. "I don't think I caught your name."

"That is because I didn't tell you." She smiled and turned to Arnold and Jensen, who both chuckled quietly. "I am guessing you didn't come here for small talk, so what can I do for you? If you want details, then I only have very few. The bodies just came in."

"I understand." Arnold walked closer. "I am just wondering if we could take a look at the two latest victims. I think the names are …"

"Alice and Trish," Iversen chimed in. "According to the list, they were given numbers eight and five."

Dijana looked through her own list but shook her head.

"I don't have number eight here, Alice. She went to central, but number five is right here." She pointed to the body under the white sheet in front of her. "I was just about to begin her autopsy."

"Iversen, could you make sure that Alice is brought over here?" Iversen nodded. "I'd prefer if you were the one to do the autopsy on both, as they seem to be the latest victims. For now, we will be focusing our investigation on them, and it's easier if they are collected in the same place."

Dijana nodded and returned to the body in front of her.

"I understand. Now let's focus on what we have. Gentlemen, meet Trish." She pulled the sheet gently from the body, and the three men stepped closer.

"Beautiful woman," Jensen noted. "But you are right, Buch; she seems to be at least in her late forties."

Arnold didn't hear him; his heart was roaring in his ears, and he felt his chest tighten like someone stabbed his heart. His right arm reached for a small table for support, but it was on wheels and started rolling when he put weight on it. The pain tightened further, and he fell to the floor, unable to speak or move.

"Buch," Jensen exclaimed and rushed to his friend's side, while it took Iversen another second to react. "Arnold, hey, look at me. Just keep calm. I think you are having a heart attack."

"Good thing we are in a hospital, then," Iversen tried. Jensen was about to kick him, when Arnold lost consciousness, and instead, he worried for his friend.

A steady beeping sound met Arnold when he woke. Bright lights illuminated the room, and it took his eyes a second to adjust. The room around him was empty, and he felt his body heavy as he sighed and relaxed into the bed. That is when he saw the ceiling and from there noticed the machines around him. He looked down over himself and found cables sticking out from his shirt. His finger had a clip on it, and a needle was secured in his hand. He groaned as he reached for his nose and felt the oxygen line. *Hospital*, he thought. *What the hell happened?*

He didn't get much further in his thoughts before a familiar face entered the room.

"Arnold, my love." Annelise hurried to his side and peppered gentle kisses all over his face. "You had me so worried. Don't you ever do that again, you hear me?"

He nodded slowly and felt her tears on his arm, as she hugged him tightly.

"Wha-a—" He coughed, and Annelise helped him raise the bed a little and handed him some water. "Thank you." His voice was raspy and weak. "Wh-what happened?"

"You, my love, were working too hard. You were in the morgue yesterday with Jensen and Iversen when you had a heart attack." She started digging through the bags she had brought in. "I feared this was coming. But not to worry. I have already spoken with Jensen, and you will, of course, take the next two weeks off to recover. We both know he will try to contact you about the case, but I warned him not to. So you can just relax and enjoy an early retirement."

"What?" Arnold exclaimed and started coughing again.

"The kids are already at home, and they are so looking forward to seeing you. The girls are taking care of the food, and your son finished the chores that you failed to do yesterday, so no need to worry about that." She was tugging at the duvet around him, and a few tears rolled over her cheeks. "You had me worried, my dear. I almost had a heart attack just thinking about what could have happened to you. But now you are home, and I have you safe for all of Christmas." Arnold had only heard half of it, his mind stilled focused on the task at hand.

"Where is my phone?" he asked and tried to sit up.

"Arnold," Annelise warned; she tried but knew it was for nothing and handed him his phone before he hurt himself trying to get out of bed.

"Jensen?" Arnold said into the phone. Jensen started taking and sounded relieved to hear his friend's voice, but Arnold interrupted him. "We need to talk. The girl in the morgue, I recognised her. Trish, I know who she is."

CHAPTER 5

It was Saturday, grocery day. Nate had driven them to the shop as always, and as per usual, he was standing around outside, smoking and talking on his phone, while Linda and Tucker took care of the shopping. He didn't like supermarkets; too many people, he said. Linda didn't mind; she and Tucker had their shopping routine, and Nate was not part of it. It also made her job a lot easier to do, and with Christmas around the corner, the shops were filled, extra people to hide behind.

"Jenny!" Linda didn't react at first. Had forgotten that this was her name now. "Jenny, Jenny! I got the trolly," Tucker shouted with a big grin on his face as he raced it towards her. He could barely reach the handlebar, and his bright smile and brown eyes peeked out from the side of the trolly.

"Aye, aye, Captain." Linda smiled back and held the trolly steady as Tucker climbed up and placed himself on his knees in the front.

"Yo, ho, out to sea we go."

He drew his wooden sabre from his belt and pointed it up in the air as he adjusted the black patch over his eye. Linda laughed for herself, her heart filling with warmth in the presence of this little boy. He was always smiling and laughing, and Linda feared the day when he would be old enough to realise the kind of world he lived in, the kind of life he would be forced into. He was too pure and joyful for the life he had ahead of him. *I will get you out of this, even if it's the last thing I do*, Linda thought to herself and shook the thoughts away, focusing on their pirate cruise.

They made their way around the store like usual. Tucker grabbed the ingredients off the shelves, and Linda crossed them from the shopping list. They had almost finished when they reached the aisle with taste samples. This week, the shop was offering them a taste of cheese. Linda had expected something Christmassy, but she figured it was in preparation for New Year's Eve, trying to inspire them to buy cheese for a late-night snack.

Captain Tucker quickly called out an order to set anchor so they could taste the cheese. He greeted the salesman and took a sample. The salesman was always the same, and he always had a new joke prepared for Tucker, one the little boy would repeat throughout the whole week, till the next shopping trip, where he would then get a new joke. One time, the salesman had repeated one of his old jokes, and Tucker had called him out on it, being able to remember all the jokes he had previously been told. *Fascinating mind in that little boy.* And the salesman had never repeated a joke again.

While the salesman kept Tucker busy, Linda quickly dropped an envelope into the bin and took a sample. They chatted for a bit and then made their way to the till.

Another smooth handover, Linda thought and felt her shoulders ease up a bit. This had been an important one. There was a big operation going down, and she had managed to gather a lot of intel. It hadn't been easy, but now she had done her bit. Taken photos and delivered them safely; the rest was up to the police. She just hoped it would be enough this time, that she would finally get out of this and be able to go back to her life again.

"Hello, hello, Captain. That is some pirate ship you have there," the cashier lady said with a bright smile. Tucker smiled just as bright and stood tall in the front of the trolly, while Linda loaded groceries onto the belt.

"I am not really a pirate," Tucker whispered. "It is just for fun."

The cashier winked at him in return, which made him beam even brighter, like they now shared a bond over this secret.

After they exited the store and parked the trolly, Tucker rushed over to the car and waved his sword in front of his dad, demanding that he join the crew and let him take his ship (the ship being his car).

"Not now, Tucker, just get in the car. We are late," Nate said and returned to his phone. Tucker hung his head and climbed into the back of the car.

"You know, it wouldn't kill you to play along just this once," Linda said firmly, as she loaded the groceries into the car, forgetting for a second who she was and clearly overstepping. Nate got off the phone and turned to her with a stern look on his face.

How dare she talk back to me? he thought. His fists were tight, and he was about to say something, when he caught Tucker's eyes peeking at them through the back window.

"You better thank him later, bitch, cause he just saved you from a beating," he spat through his teeth and made a gesture towards the car. Linda swallowed hard and got in the car without saying another word.

The ride back was quiet. No one said anything; no one moved. When they got home, Tucker ran off to his room, while Linda prepared herself for what was to come.

She went into the kitchen, put away the groceries, and started to prepare their dinner. She was rinsing the salad greens when she heard his steps coming up behind her. She knew what was going to happen before it even did. Nate grabbed her hair tightly and yanked it back as he forced her down on the kitchen counter.

"You thought I forgot about you, didn't you?" He laughed and pushed her jeans down. "I thought you had learned to obey me, but I guess you need a little more convincing." He ripped her shirt and bit her shoulder, as if to mark her and remind her that she was just property. His property. Linda shut her eyes and prayed that Tucker stayed in his room. He didn't deserve to see this. He adored his dad, and this would crush him.

She covered her mouth as the pain rushed over her and stood still in hopes that it would be over quickly. *Be quiet, Hemmer. Tucker cannot hear you.* She tried to distract her mind. She had been raped before; with Nate, it was a common occurrence, but she had also been raped before that. The first time was when she had just been a child. She hadn't been more than six or seven years old, and every time it had happened since, she had crawled back in time and felt like she was that little girl again, going through this for the first time all over again.

He placed his arm around her neck, and she had to gasp for air. Her eyes flew open, and for a second, she thought, *This is it; I am going to die now.* But then he had removed his arm again, and she started coughing in relief of being able to breathe again.

Her eyes caught a squirrel running around in the garden. It moved quickly over the tall grass and seemed to be carrying something as it crawled its way up the tree and disappeared between the branches. *I thought they hibernated during wintertime,* Linda wondered and looked closer at the tree to relocate her little friend. Just like he could sense that she didn't want to go through this alone, he popped his head up again and seemed to be staring straight at her. *Help me.* She couldn't help the thought, but she knew it was a waste of energy. If she didn't satisfy Nate, then he would just send her elsewhere, and then there would be no one left to take care of Tucker.

Her thoughts got interrupted as she felt her body get pulled back off the kitchen counter and thrown onto the floor. He kept her pinned on her stomach and pulled her jeans farther down before he climbing back on top of her. He started grunting, and Linda found comfort in knowing that it would be over soon. Just as she finished the thought, she felt him collapse on top of her, his breath warm and heavy on her neck.

"See," he whispered and pulled her head back by her hair. "I own you, bitch, and don't you forget it."

He removed himself and grabbed a beer from the fridge before heading into his office.

Linda was shaking as she pushed herself up by her arms and slowly made her way to the bathroom. It wasn't until she closed the door that she allowed herself to cry. Her entire body trembling as she slid down the door and sat on the cold tiled floor.

Her hand muffled her cries and then grabbed some paper when she broke the skin. *Get it together, Hemmer; get it together.* She took a few deep breaths, got up from the floor, and cleaned herself with trembling hands, noticing from the mirror view that she would have to find a scarf or something to cover up the bruising. She carefully walked to the bedroom and found a long-neck sweater.

Just as she finished up, a gentle knock sounded on the door, and Tucker's bright face poked in. His smile was all the strength she needed to push through and ignore the pain, the hurt, and the fear. She smiled back at him and grabbed his hand as they made their way to the kitchen to continue making dinner.

Later, Tucker went to get his dad, and they all sat down to have dinner like nothing had happened, like they were just a normal family. Anyone looking in wouldn't know what had just happened. They would just see a normal family, a child with his mother and father. They would make that conclusion without knowing that Linda was not Tucker's mother and that Tucker's real mother had been sold into prostitution after giving birth. They wouldn't know that Tucker's farther was a criminal and a part of an organisation which kidnapped women and children, and sold them off as property to the highest bidders. They wouldn't know that Linda was there as an undercover police officer to gather enough information on the operation to finally put an end to this nightmare.

To the unknown eye, they looked just like any other family.

Linda felt sick. Her stomach turned, and she had to excuse herself.

"Jenny, are you okay?" Tucker asked and was about to follow her, when his father stopped him and told him to stay put. "But Jenny is—"

"Shut it, kid," Nate snapped, taking a deep breath as he kept cutting his steak.

Tucker kept quiet and slumped back down in his seat. Linda heard the exchange and dreamt of the day where she could take Tucker away from here. She might not have given birth to him, but for the past year and a half, she had been his mother. She had been the one to tuck him in at night and hold him close, so he felt safe. She had been the one to kiss away his bruises when he got hurt, or laugh and smile with him when they were playing. She had been the one to make him dinners and give him baths and made sure he had everything he needed. She had been there for him every day, and she would continue to be. The only thing she was regretting was not being there sooner.

She threw some water on her face and went back into the kitchen. Tucker smiled at the sight of her, and she kissed him gently on top of his head.

"I am better now," she whispered to him and gave his little hand a reassuring squeeze as she sat back down to let the charade continue.

CHAPTER 6

"Jenny, Jenny, Jenny," a happy voice sounded through the wall. Linda heard it faintly but quickly found herself dozing off again, pulled back into her dream as sleep kept a tight hold of her. "Jenny! Jenny, wake up." The little voice was closer now. The door to her bedroom swung open, and Tucker jumped onto her bed. Linda stayed still and pretended to be asleep. "Wake up, Jenny. Wake up."

His tiny fingers danced over her face, stroking her cheeks. Linda saw her shot and jumped up from the bed. Tucker giggled and squealed as he dove under the duvet, and then a tickle war broke out.

They spent most of the morning in bed, reading books and playing Ludo.

Sunday mornings were her favourite time. Nate always left very early for work, and he always came home very late in the evening or sometimes even the next day. That left Linda alone with Tucker, and for a short time, they could pretend that everything was okay, that they were safe, and that it was just a normal Sunday. A normal weekend for a normal family. Just a mother and son spending some quality time together.

"What do you say champ; do you want to go for a walk? Maybe we could go to the park or the beach. What do you say?" Linda asked, and Tucker looked up at her with serious eyes.

"Are we allowed?" he asked.

Linda felt her chest tighten. *Are we allowed? Oh, sweet child. You deserve a life where you can go the beach or park whenever you want. You deserve to be free, my boy. I will make sure you get free.*

"Of course, we are allowed. I will take care of it, okay?" She ruffled his hair and pinched his cheek, sparking a faint smile on his face. "Go brush your teeth and put on some clothes, okay? Then I will call your dad and tell him where we are going." Tucker nodded and seemed excited as he ran off to his room.

Linda found her phone and hovered over Nate's name. He hated it when she called him during business hours. Last time she did, he came home and broke her ribs. She hadn't been allowed to go to the hospital, hadn't been allowed to rest, and she could still feel how her ribs were misplaced. They were still pushing on her lung. She hated to think what would happen this time around. *So much for a day in the park*, she thought and called him.

The phone kept ringing and went to voicemail. She tried again, but still no answer. "Pick up, you bastard," she whispered, but the phone just kept ringing.

She thought about leaving, just going to the park and having a nice day, but she knew they would be followed, and she would be in trouble if they just left.

"I am ready." Tucker smiled as he appeared in her door. "Aren't you getting dressed?"

Linda put her brave face on and smiled happily at him.

"Of course, I am. Go watch some TV, and I will get ready in the meantime."

Tucker nodded eagerly and ran off to the living room.

Only one option left. She didn't like this, but it was better than leaving without letting anyone know. She dialled another number and waited for a response.

"Hey, Gregg, it's Jenny. I know I shouldn't be calling you, and I am sorry to trouble you. I have tried calling Nate, but he is not answering. Yes, I know I shouldn't be calling him, either. The thing is, Tucker and I would like to go to the park. And I would like your permission." The line went quiet, though she could hear Gregg's breathing. "Gregg, do I have your permission to go to the park with Tucker? You can send a team with me. We just want to go to the playground for a bit, maybe get a burger."

"Jenny, are you ready yet? Did you talk to Dad?" Tucker yelled from the living room.

"Sorry, that is just Tucker. He is ready to leave, waiting for me for me to get ready." *Please say yes; please say yes. Please, please, please.* Her shoulders relaxed when a single "Yes" had sounded on the phone and the line went dead. "Thank you! Thank you," she whispered to no one and hurried to the bathroom to get ready. She pushed the worries aside. Consequences be damned; they were an issue for later.

The park was quiet. They almost had the place to themselves. They were playing on the swings, jumping off and pretending to be airplanes.

"I am flying, Jenny, look. I am flying," Tucker shouted and jumped off the swing as it went forward.

Linda worried that he might get too brave, swing a little too high and get hurt, but he just rolled on the ground as he landed, just like she had taught him. Just like they had planned, in case they had to run away. She had debated with herself on whether it was necessary or not, but concluded that it was. It was a tough life lesson to teach a six-year-old. Hell, it was a tough life lesson to teach anyone. She loved that little boy, and she would do anything to keep him safe. Anything and everything.

They lived on the second floor. There was a small jump from his window onto the roof of the garage below. From there was a bigger jump to the ground, a jump that could break his legs if he didn't do it properly, so she had to teach him. Her heart had dropped to her stomach the first time he had leaped from the roof. They had practiced on the swings before, practiced on boxes in the garage, from the counter in the kitchen, and from the smaller roof of the bike shed. He had landed it every time, like a champ, and followed all her instructions. He had done so well, and she didn't doubt him for a second. Or that is what she had told him, and herself, though when he had leaped off the real building, her heart had stopped. She wondered if it had all been a mistake, if she had pushed him too hard, gone a little too far. If it had even been necessary, but all her worry had been for nothing. Tucker landed the jump perfectly, and Linda had never been prouder.

"That was really great, Tucker," Linda cheered and swung him around in the air. "What do you say to burgers? Could you eat a burger?"

Tucker nodded and pulled her towards the swings.

"Just one more jump."

Linda laughed and joined him on the swings again.

"Ready for takeoff, Captain?" she asked, and Tucker nodded. "Okay, switching on the engine."

"Engine switched on," Tucker repeated and started swinging.

He quickly got higher and higher, and Linda was swinging by his side. They shared a look and started counting down.

"Three, two, one, now!" They laughed and leaped into the air.

Kept laughing as they rolled around on the ground.

"What do you want us to do, boss?" Gregg released a breath and flicked his cigarette onto the ground.

"Nothing," he said simply and took one last look at Jenny and Tucker. "Keep an eye on them, but don't intervene. Stay back; don't let them see you." The guys around him gave a simple nod, and he made his way to the car.

"Boss, you sure about this?" a deep voice asked from the front seat.

Gregg stifled a laugh.

"I don't recall asking for your opinion."

"Sorry, boss."

"Don't apologise. Just keep your mouth shut. If I want your opinion, trust me, I will ask for it."

"Sure thing, boss."

Gregg hummed.

"Let's get out of here. Oh, and give Nate a call. Seems like I have a thing or two to teach that man. This is no way to treat family. I have had it with his bullshit. Tucker is a great kid, and Jenny has been a great mother for him. The least that man can do is answer his fucking phone when they call. Or take a day off, be a dad for once in his pathetic fucking life."

With bellies filled with milkshakes and burgers, they made their way home.

As they approached the bus stop, Linda heard someone shouting her name. Her heart leaped into her throat at the sound, looking for a way out as she recognised the voice.

"Linda. Linda," a woman called out.

Linda tightened her hold on Tucker's hand and braced herself for the confrontation. She looked around and prayed that Gregg's people were not following them. Being recognised could ruin everything.

"Linda, wait up," the woman shouted.

Like faith heard her, the bus pulled up, and she quickly lifted Tucker onto the step, and they got onto the bus. The doors closed before the woman reached them.

"I'm sorry," Linda mouthed to the woman as their eyes locked through the window. The bus started moving, but they never once broke eye contact till it picked up speed, and the woman was out of sight. "I'm sorry," Linda whispered again and closed her eyes.

She felt her heart ache, and a tear rolled down her chin. *Andrea*. Her mind raced. All she wanted for so long was to see her again, hear her voice again, and there she was. She was right there, right there. Andrea had called her name, and Linda had recognised it instantly. Oh, how she wanted to run back and embrace the woman in her arms. hold her close, just for a while. More tears fell, and she just now understood how much she needed a hug, how much she craved a sense of security, someone to take care of her for once.

"It's okay," Tucker said softly and squeezed her hand tighter. Linda forced a smile and wrapped her arm around him. "Why are you sad?"

"It is nothing, my love. It is nothing for you to worry about. Grownups just get sad sometimes." Tucker wrapped his little arms around her, held her tight, and looked up at her with his big brown eyes.

"I will help you feel better, Mom. You always help me; let me help you now." *Mom*, Linda thought; *he just called me Mom*. Her whole face broke into a wide smile as she kissed the top of his head.

"You always make me feel better, honey. Always."

"I love you, Mom," he whispered, and Linda didn't think her heart could take more.

"I love you too, sweetheart. I love you too, so much."

CHAPTER 7

Linda sat in the shower, shaking and watching as the blood ran down her thigh and followed the water into the drain. She closed her eyes and took a deep breath. Focused on the sensations. The ice-cold water hit her skin like daggers, and her head was pounding. Her lips were trembling as she drew short breaths. Her body slowly started to feel numb. The cuts on her thigh burned nicely, like it was the only feeling she had left.

She cried, not for herself but for everyone else. Everyone in her life seemed to suffer because of her. She always tried to do the right thing, but someone always got hurt. She didn't doubt for a second that everyone was better off without her. If it wasn't for Tucker, she would have ended it right there. Parts of her still considered it, wondered if Tucker was better off as well. He probably was. But she was his ticket out of here. Without her, he would never get away. She had to get him somewhere safe first. Make sure he was taken care of, and then she could give up on herself. If she could get him out of here, then he could get a nice new family. He could go to school and get actual friends. He could be happy.

She cut another line in her thigh and felt the buzz fill her mind. Her body stopped shaking, and all her muscles relaxed. *Who knew pain could be such a drug?*

Tears kept rolling down her face, but she didn't feel them. The cold water had made her face numb. The only thing she felt was the cuts on her thighs. She released a breath and dropped the blade on the floor. Her hand had started shaking again, and she couldn't hold onto it anymore.

As if she hadn't already put herself through enough, she found her mind wandering back in time, searching for any memory that could cause her pain. Knocking over her neatly packed boxes with emotions she had stored away and long forgotten about, feelings and memories she had stuffed down so deep, they barely existed anymore. For a year and a half, she had been hiding behind a mask, pretending to be someone else. But one could only hide for so long. One could only store away so many boxes before they all came tumbling down. She felt it happening; she was losing her mind, losing control. *Just a few more days. I just need to keep it together for a few more days.* She had to keep fighting; she had to hold on for just a little bit longer. Tucker needed her. He had called her Mom, and he needed her.

The funeral had brought up so many memories, and seeing Andrea, hearing her voice, just made it worse. Now, all she could think about was Andrea and Willa, and the life they used to have. There were so many beautiful memories, so many wonderful times she had promised she would cherish forever. Now, all those moments that once had made her laugh and smile, they all just brought her pain. Made her angry. So she had stored them away, kept them hidden, and pretended like they didn't even exist, like it had never happened.

She opened her eyes and felt her body stiff as she got up to turn off the water. She cleaned herself with a towel and put the blade back in her razor. The last blood washed down the drain as the water stopped flooding. She wrapped herself in a towel and put her game-face back on.

"Just a few more days," she whispered to herself and looked in the mirror. She barely recognised the reflection staring back at her, and honestly, she was surprised Andrea had been able to recognise her. She had lost a lot of weight, her muscles even more prominent than usual, making her face bonier and sharper. Her eyes looked bigger, and her shoulders looked broader.

She let the towel fall and took a long look at herself. She used to be able to turn heads when she walked in a crowd. Could never sit alone at the bar, and would always have someone random come up to her on the street. She doubted she'd be able to turn any heads now, and if she did, it would probably be out of pity or worry for how ragged she looked.

Bruises covered her body from head to toe. The woman in the mirror looked tired, defeated. She didn't look like a police officer. She didn't look like a soldier.

But the woman in the mirror was her. She might not recognise herself, but it was her. She turned around, her back facing the mirror, and slowly turned her head to look at herself. There it was, the confirmation. The woman in the mirror was indeed her. She closed her eyes and turned away. Walked to the bedroom and got dressed. Made sure to put on enough layers to hide the scarring on her back. She was always terrified that someone would be able to feel it through her clothes. She didn't know how, but so far, she had been able to hide her scars from Nate and the rest of the gang. None of them had actually seen her naked. They had all mostly been too busy fucking her to even consider undressing her properly. Or they had been too drunk to see anything at all.

Tucker had seen them once. He had walked in on her while she was getting dressed.

"Wings," he had said. "You have wings."

It hadn't been a question so much as an observation. She had told him a story about a guardian angel, one that Gran had told her after she had come home from school crying after gym class. The other kids had made fun of her because of her scars, asked her if she could fly, and pushed her around on the playground.

Back then, she hadn't been able to remember why she had the scars or how she had even gotten them in the first place. She remembered bits and pieces now, but still not all. Therapists had told her that she had done it to herself. Maybe they were right. Through therapy and hypnosis, she had remembered how her skin on her back had felt like acid, and she had tried to cut it off. Only being able to reach so far, she had cut from the middle and towards her shoulders on both sides, unintentionally making it look like wings on her back.

Some memories conflicted with others. What she really remembered was that her friend had done it for her. He had cut her back upon her request. She had asked him to make the pain go away. But the boy didn't exist; he wasn't real. She had done it to herself; that is what the therapist had told her. Her mind had made up the boy as a ploy to cover for her self-harm.

She pushed the memories aside and went to bed, covering herself under the duvet and hoping Nate wouldn't return till morning.

A scream woke her from her sleep, and she instinctively ran to Tucker's room. He was shrieking and kicking his covers off in his sleep. Linda gently put her hand on his chest and whispered his name till his eyes met hers.

"It's okay, sweetheart; it's just a nightmare. It's not real."

Tucker cried quietly and crawled into her lap, hugging her close.

"I'm scared, Mom."

"Shh, it's okay. I got you; you are safe. I am here."

She hugged him back and lay down on the bed with him, still clinging to her like a baby monkey. She drew soothing circles on his back and started humming a melody that came to her out of nowhere. "Mmm mm mm mm, m-mm mm mmm mm m-mm." She didn't know the song, but somehow the melody felt familiar and calming. Tucker seemed to think the same and quickly fell back asleep, his hands still gripping Linda's shirt tightly.

Linda herself was about to doze off when she was pulled back awake by a hand covering her mouth and her body being yanked from the bed. Her instincts told her to fight back, but then she looked over at Tucker, who was still asleep, and she instead just let it happen. Let it take her. Hoping that whatever *it* was, it would happen somewhere else away from the sleeping boy. Somewhere safe from disrupting his sleep.

She was pulled by her hair out of the room and down the hallway. She thought they were headed to the bedroom, when she felt a hard kick at her side, and she tumbled down the stairs. She tried to brace herself, covered her head, and felt her wrist snap as it got caught in an angle between her body and the stairs. Her lungs betrayed her, and she yelped out in pain, before she fell to the ground floor and laid still, breathing slowly as she tried to recover. Her hand now covering her wrist and tugging it tightly to her chest.

"That is what you get, bitch," Nate spat. He pulled her up by her hair and positioned a gun at her head. "You see this?" he asked, flicking the gun towards his face. He was bruised. His left eye was all swollen and bloody. *Is he missing a tooth?* "You did this. You and that bastard kid."

She started to protest, tell him Tucker had nothing to do with it, but when she opened her mouth to speak, the gun was shoved inside, and she froze. If he shot her now, there would be no telling what he would do with Tucker.

"Nate ... mhmp." She tried speaking, but he just pushed the gun farther down her throat, and she felt herself gag.

"Shut up, you fucking cunt," he screamed and tossed her to the ground. "You went to Gregg? What did you tell him, huh?" He kicked her till she spat up blood. He put the gun down on a little table by the stairs; he needed both hands to finish this. Oh, how he was going to enjoy this. He smiled as he grabbed her hair again and dragged her into the kitchen.

She was on her back on the floor with his hands tightly around her neck. She tried to stay calm. Assess the situation and get out of this. She knew how; she had been trained for this, but her body wouldn't move. Her arms just laid slack alongside her body.

He had a determined look in his eyes. He was going to kill her.

She could hold her breath for a long time, longer than the average person, but he was probably going to crush her neck before then. She closed her eyes and prayed that Tucker would have heard the yelling and escaped through the window like they had practiced. *That innocent little boy. I am sorry, Tucker.*

A gunshot rang through room.

Linda's eyes snapped open at the sound. Her heart panicked, thinking Nate brought someone with him. *Tucker! No, no, no, no. No!* She couldn't lose another child. She couldn't.

"Tucker," she shrieked with a muffled sound and felt blood dripping on her as the hold on her neck loosened. Nate fell heavily on her. She wasn't sure if it was his or her blood that started spilling on the floor. It all happened so quickly. The gunshot, the blood, and Nate's body. She pushed him off and crawled away, panting heavily and coughing. She cried as she tried to breathe. Then she saw it, the gun. "Tucker," she whispered.

The little boy was standing in the doorway with the gun held high, his little hands trembling from what he had just done.

"Oh, Tucker," Linda cried and got up. "It is okay, sweetheart." Her voice was shaken and hoarse, like her throat was still struggling to expand again. "Sweetheart, give me the gun, yeah. Just give it to me." She slowly put her hand on his holding the gun. "Just let it go, it is okay. It's okay." Tucker started crying and shaking; he let go of the gun.

"He-he was h-hurting you." Tucker wept, and Linda's heart fell to her stomach. She wrapped the boy up in a tight hug and cried with him. "Is-is he-he dead?" *Yes.* But she couldn't say that, could she?

"Tucker, look at me." She wrapped his face in her hands and winced a little from the pain in her wrist. "Look at me, sweetheart." She smiled at him and met his eyes with a gentle look. "You are such a brave boy. This was not your fault, okay? You are right; your dad was hurting me, but he will not do that anymore. Do you hear me? We are safe now, okay?"

Tucker nodded quietly and kept looking into her eyes.

This is my fault. It should never have gotten this far. I should have gotten you out of here a long time ago.

Tucker's fingers carefully danced over her cheek and stopped at the bruise left under her eye. "I am okay," Linda said and took his hands in hers. "I am okay," she repeated and rested her forehead against his. "You are okay. We are both okay. We are safe." She kept repeating it while they cried. "Repeat it with me."

"Y-you okay, mm, I'm okay. We-we s-s-safe," Tucker stuttered.

"Again."

"Y-you okay, I'm okay. We are safe."

"Again."

CHAPTER 8

Arnold still had hospital tape on his hand when entering the station. He had barely managed to tuck in his shirt in his hurry to get there.

His phone call with Jensen had been cut short, when his phone had run out of battery, and he had seen no other option than to leave the hospital against medical advice. Annelise had just let him. She knew her husband and knew there was no point in fighting him on this, though she was now really looking forward to his retirement. She just hoped that he would take care of himself long enough to make it that far. He had always jumped headfirst into danger and not considered his own safety. It had resulted in some close calls throughout the years, but this heart attack had really stirred a scary feeling in the pit of her stomach.

She wanted him to slow down, but he just continued his very determined stroll through the halls of the station. "Arnold, slow down," she called. "Please, love, just wait a second; you are walking too fast." She had caught up with him but doubted that he was even listening. "Arnold Elijah Buch! You stop right now."

Arnold stopped in his tracks and snapped out of the trance he was in and turned to his wife. *Fury* did not even come close to cover the look that was in her eyes. She took a deep breath, stepped closer, and put her hands on his face. Her voice softened, and so did her eyes.

"Love, I know you need to do this. I know you cannot rest till this is solved. I know you, and I love you. So I beg of you, please, please be careful. Please remember to breathe and take a break." She caressed his face and gave him a tender look. "But most importantly, remember to come home." She kissed him briefly and started tucking his shirt and straightening his tie. "I need you, my love. There will always be a case. There will always be a murder out there, always. You won't have enough time to catch them all, and that is okay. But if you don't take care of yourself, then you will have even less time, and you and I, we won't have any time left at all."

She is right, he thought.

"I am sorry, Annelise," he stated simply, not knowing really what else he should say.

"I know. I know." She finished fixing his tie and then caught his eyes again. "Now, if this watch here beeps, you are to sit down and not move till your pulse is low enough again."

"Annelise," he tried to protest, but his wife stopped him before he could continue.

"No. This is not up for discussion. It is your job to solve this case, and I understand that. But I am your wife, and we made a promise to always take care of each other. So I am telling you, when this watch beeps, you will sit down and not move."

She gave him another quick peck and turned to leave. Arnold took a deep breath and looked at the modern technology around his wrist. *102 beats per minute*, he read. He took another deep breath and slowed his walk. Figured Annelise was right; she usually was.

"Buch, what are you doing here?" Iversen's voice cut through, and he felt the young man tap his shoulder.

"Find Jensen please, will you? I need to speak with both of you." He saw Iversen nod and disappear down the hall. He looked at the watch again. 95 bpm. *I can do this*. He looked at the coffee machine and smelled the beans before deciding against it, making himself a cup of hot water and grabbed a scoop of herbal tea. *Herbal tea. If a heart attack won't be the end of me, then this tea will*. He hummed to himself and went into the conference room.

"Buch, there you are. I was wondering how long they'd be able to keep you at the hospital." Jensen embraced his lifelong friend in a brief hug. "I bet Annelise is not thrilled about you being here."

Arnold made a hand gesture, and Jensen didn't push the topic any further. He knew his friend well enough to know when some topic was off base. Sometimes exchanging a look was all it took for them to get the hint. That's why it only took one look from Arnold for Jensen to understand that he had not yet processed it all and neither had Annelise, so he decided to change the subject. Started to give an update on the case, instead.

"Our phone call got cut short, and I didn't quite understand what you were saying. But you mentioned the victim, Trish?"

"Yes, you said you knew who she was?" Iversen cut in and sat down, resting his feet on the desk.

Jensen gave him a sombre side look, and the young man quickly retracted his feet again and put them on the ground. Arnold chuckled quietly and shook his head, remembering their younger days where himself and Jensen had shown the same level of overconfidence. They had gotten into so much trouble. Both had even gotten suspended at one point: insubordination. They had been close to losing their jobs, and now here they were. Jensen was in charge and on top of his career, and Arnold was on his way to retirement as one of the most respected people in their field.

If you said the name Arnold Buch, the whole station knew who you were talking about. Everyone had a story to tell where he had been involved in a case. Even if they hadn't been there at the time, they would still have heard a story. Arnold had a feeling this case would turn into another one of those stories.

"That's right; I know who Trish is. Or I am pretty sure I do. But we need to go to the morgue again before I can be 100 percent sure. I'll need to see her again."

There was much more activity in the morgue this time. Many bodies were on display, and everyone working had a heavy look on their faces. Dijana asked her colleagues to clear the room when she saw the trio arrive. Her colleagues didn't seem to mind the break. They still had a lot to do, but the magnitude of it all was just overwhelming, and they had to take their time, if they were to get through it all.

"Gentlemen, welcome back," Dijana said and rested her eyes in Arnold. "Good to see you are still standing, Buch; you had us all worried there for a second."

Arnold gave her a reassuring smile and stepped towards the table where the body lay.

"Oh, Trish," he whispered, resting his hands on the table near her shoulder.

"So, you do know her?" Iversen asked, and Arnold nodded.

"Yes." His answer was brief before he fell into silence once more. He had met Trish once before. She had shouted at him and hit him, after her little sister had gotten into an accident. It wasn't the first time someone had let their anger and frustrations out on him, and it definitely wasn't the last. He probably would not have remembered her if it hadn't been for her sister, Linda. The two of them looked so much alike, it was almost scary.

If he remembered correctly, there were three sisters, and they all looked alike, but Trish and Linda especially. Last time he was in the morgue and had seen Trish's body, he thought it was Linda, and it was like his whole world had come crashing down.

He had never been good at keeping his work and private life separate, but he had always tried his best not to get overly invested in the victims' lives. With Linda, he had failed at that. She had stolen his heart from the very second he had laid eyes on her. His fatherly heart had melted.

"Who is she, then?" Iversen asked, breaking the silence.

"Hemmer, Trish Hemmer," Arnold replied and felt a tear run over his cheek.

"She is not on the list," Iversen said. "There is no Hemmer anywhere on the list. Are you absolutely sure it is her?" Arnold nodded. "There is a Trisha Evans mentioned on the list. Maybe the name 'Trish' on the white stone is referring to her? How do you know this is Trish Hemmer?"

"I spoke with her around three years ago," Arnold replied. "She showed up shouting at me in my office. I will never forget the anger on her face." He chuckled quietly to himself. "I know it is her; she and her sister look alike, and I saw them both at their grandmother's funeral just last week."

"But she is not on any of the lists," Iversen repeated.

"Maybe her family has not reported her missing yet." Jensen's voice cut through. "And you are sure, Buch?"

"Yes." Arnold didn't hesitate for a second. He was sure. He looked down at Tish's body again. "Don't you recognise her yourself?" he asked, and Jensen stepped closer. "Imagine her with brown hair and about fifteen years younger. Facial features are the same, but imagine her body much more toned, and her shoulders a lot broader. Doesn't she remind you of someone?"

Jensen hummed and looked closer.

"A deep scar across her forehead and eye," Arnold continued, tracing his finger down over her brow and left eye. They were quiet for a minute before Jensen stepped back and looked at his friend.

"Good God, why did that take me so long? You even gave me the name," Jensen mumbled, shocked. "Hemmer. This is her sister."

"Sorry, who are we talking about?" Iversen asked and stepped closer to the body.

"She's one of us," Arnold explained. "She is a police officer. You wouldn't have met her; she changed department years ago and spends most of her time on undercover operations."

Silence fell over them again as they watched over the woman for a minute. Arnold was the first one to move. He motioned for Dijana to come closer and for Iversen to move out of the way.

"What's her name?" Iversen asked, this time a bit louder. He looked at his two colleagues for a minute before reluctantly moving away and giving space to Dijana.

"They have the same tattoo," Arnold said. "Trish showed me that day when she yelled at me. She was upset that I was sending her sister away on another mission. She had only just come back from one, and they had all missed her terribly. I tried to find someone else, but she was really the only one." He lifted Trish's arm and turned it, displaying a spiral tattooed on her wrist. "The ancient spirals represent the winding journey inward we must take if we are to truly know and love ourselves. From that journey, we return with more power and wisdom." He traced the spiral with his index finger and closed his eyes for a minute, wanting to honour those words. "It is a symbol of rebirth."

At that, Iversen snapped his head up.

"Rebirth?" he asked, and Arnold nodded. "Why rebirth?"

"You know young people these days; they read an interesting quote somewhere and get it tattooed. Maybe it is not a sign of rebirth but more a symbol of spiralling out of control. Or maybe just a simple spiral?" Jensen suggested, but Arnold shook his head.

"No, it is the spirituality spiral. The ancient sign of rebirth. The proof that when something starts, it never stops. One small action, comment, or thought turns into more and more. It just continues into infinity. We get born, we live, we die. Our life is remembered, and people mourn us. Our spirits learn from the past and develop again, until we are reborn. One continuous cycle. A spiral."

Arnold went quiet and started walking around the room. Continued to talk about spirituality and past lives, while Iversen and Jensen exchanged a look, figured this was just another one of his usual rants. Iversen had found it unbelievably annoying in the beginning, but now it was kind of endearing. It was like an elderly person, trying to make sense of the world. Arnold would have a field day if he ever found out that Iversen viewed him that way. The thought made the younger man chuckle, and he got side-eyed by Jensen again.

"Where are you going with this?" Iversen asked.

"I don't know. I was just thinking about Trish and remembered how passionate she was about their tattoo. She said it was the thing that tied them together. The one thing that no one else would understand. She said they both had been given a second chance, been reborn." He chuckled again. "She threatened me. Told me to keep her little sister safe or else she would come find me and make my life a living hell." He laughed again at the memory. "She was quite convincing, actually. Only two other people have been able to intimidate me like that: my wife and Trish's little sister."

His smile stiffened, and he looked back at Trish's body. How was he supposed to tell the family about this? How was he supposed to break that sisterly bond forever? They both might have been reborn once, but Trish was not coming back this time.

I am sorry. I was so focused on keeping your little sister safe, when you were the one in need of protection.

CHAPTER 9

Iversen was sitting on a stool, tapping his foot. He kept looking at his watch, and the pencil he held in his hand had snapped in two. They had been at the morgue for over an hour now and so far, they had been talking about spirituality and a mystery sister. They hadn't made any progress whatsoever, and the strong scent of cleaning products was starting to get to him. He felt a headache coming on, and after a while, he swore he could smell every single body in those fridge containers.

I can't take this anymore, he thought to himself and shoved the broken pencil into his pocket.

"That's enough," he yelled and stood up abruptly.

Jensen, Arnold, and Dijana all turned to him, and he chose to let it all out. Maybe venting would make him feel better.

"What are we doing here?" he asked and felt his voice echo through the room. "We haven't done anything. For the past half-hour, we've only been talking about some kind of symbol and how great Trish was at telling people off. This isn't getting us anywhere. People are dead. Young women have been murdered, and you keep talking about this sister, police officer, whatever she is, but every time I ask for more details, you just cut me off. Who is she? Who is this sister, and why is she relevant?"

He took a few deep breaths. His fists loosened, and he realised he had been puffing his chest.

"Are you done now?" Jensen asked with a raised eyebrow, and Iversen just nodded, relaxed, and sat back down on the stool.

"I am sorry, Iversen, you are right. I guess I got a bit distracted," Arnold said and took a seat next to his younger colleague. "Trish was a remarkable woman, and her sister, Linda, is just as remarkable. Not only that, but she is very important to me. Seeing Trish like this shocked me, and for a second,

I thought it was Linda. Despite the age gap, the two of them looks so much alike." He looked down and wondered again how he was ever going to tell Linda about this. "Guess I got a bit sentimental."

"Thank you for including me," Iversen said and put a hand on his shoulder. "So, Linda; guess we need to talk to her. Where is she?"

"She is not available," Arnold answered shortly and stood back up. "She is still on the assignment I sent her on. Or I assume she is. They don't really keep me in the loop; they haven't done for the past year."

"But there must be some way of contacting her, right? You said you had seen them both at a funeral last week? I mean, if she could attend that, then surely, she can take out a minute to talk with us? Or maybe you could send me in, and I could talk with her?"

Arnold hummed and started walking around the room again, like he did every time he was concentrating.

The watch on his wrist beeped, and he saw that his pulse was way too high. Annelise would have a field day if she found out. He smiled to himself as he imagined his wife telling him off, and he grabbed the nearest stool to take a seat. As he sat, Trish was right in his line of sight. It was still scary how much she and Linda looked alike. The third sister, Helen, looked more like their brother, but they all four shared the same bright-blue eyes and wide striking smile.

He felt a shiver down his spine. Seeing her like this seemed all too familiar. Suddenly his vision changed, and it was no longer the body of the fifty-three-year-old Trish that was in front of him. Instead, it was a girl, a child. She was no more than seven years old.

> It all happened in matter of minutes.
> They had broken down the door to the apartment and heard screams from upstairs. A little girl.
> Arnold had been the first one up the steps and into the bathroom, where the screams had died out. His three seconds of hesitation to pull the man away almost cost the life of a little girl. She was floating in the bathtub, lifeless. She was naked, and her lips were blue. Her little hand was resting on the bathtub edge like she had been gripping it tightly, fighting for her life just seconds ago. There was

blood in the water coming from a deep gash in the little girl's forehead across her eye.

The man standing over her did not protest as he was arrested and removed, just kept his eyes on the girl. Even when he could no longer see her, he seemed to still be looking for her. It was like he could look through the walls, kept his eyes at the same spot, knew exactly where she was.

Arnold grabbed her little body and hoisted her out of the bath, laid her down on the bathroom floor, and started CPR. He could feel her little ribs crack under his hands as he was massaging her heart. Her body moved under the force as Arnold frantically kept pumping on her chest.

"Come on," he whispered. "Come on."

His colleagues tried to stop him, told him it had already been too long, that there was nothing more to do. But then it happened: She came back. She began coughing and screaming and waving her arms and kicking her legs. Arnold grabbed her hands and held them to his chest.

"It is okay. You are okay. We are okay," he repeated and tapped her little hands with his fingers in a steady rhythm like his heart. "Breathe for me, will you?"

She nodded.

"You are okay, you are safe now. I promise you, you are safe now."

The girl nodded again and seemed to calm down.

Arnold let her hands go and grabbed a towel. "You must be cold; is it okay if I wrap this around you?"

Again, she nodded. She sat up and held the towel tight around herself, still shaking from the cold water. "My name is Arnold, can you tell me your name?" he asked and sat on the floor next to her.

"Lin- Linda," she managed, stuttering and coughing from her sore throat.

"Linda, that is a pretty name. How old are you?"

"Si- six, six and, and a half."

He smiled; the "half" was important at that age. He remembered the little candy cane he had bought for his own daughter. He felt his pockets and lifted the candy cane from it. "Do you want this?" She shook her head and hid further in the towel.

"Other … Oth- Others," she stuttered, and Arnold frowned.

"Others?"

She nodded and pointed to the door.

"Are the others here?" She nodded again. "Where are they? Can you show me?"

She nodded again and got up. Her small legs could barely support her as she ran down the stairs still with the towel around her, and Arnold following closely after. It was clear from her wobbly state and the way her body was carrying her, that she hadn't been running in a long time. Made Arnold wonder how long she had been locked up for.

She stopped at the basement door and pointed at it.

"Are they down there?"

The little girl nodded and stepped away.

Arnold called some colleagues over and motioned for them to check the basement while he took the girl with him into the kitchen.

He will never forget the scared look in her eyes or the way she held onto herself. She was way too young to have experienced so much. You could see it in her eyes; it was like she had an old soul. Years of pain and torment were painted on her face. Six years old, and she already had more suffering than most people would have in a lifetime.

Arnold made them each a cup of tea. He noticed deep scarring on her back, as he made his way around her. It looked fresh; parts of it were still bleeding. He called over one of his female colleagues and knelt down in front of the little girl.

"Linda, do you remember you told me, you are six years old?"

She nodded and then added, "And a half." Her stuttering seemed to have gone away. Progress, Arnold thought to himself.

"That is right, yes, six and a half." He smiled. "So do you know what happens if you fall and hurt your knee?" She nodded. "Can you tell me?"

"You start bleeding and will need a Band-aid. And then my big sister gives it a kiss to make it all better."

"That is right. So, you know how important it is to put a Band-aid on when you are hurt, right?" She nodded again and accepted a wet cloth to hold against her eye. The cut was deep and had to be painful, but she didn't even seem to flinch. "My friend here has some Band-aids, and we need to check if someone has hurt you. Is it okay if we look at your back?"

This time, she didn't nod right away but instead pushed the towel down herself. Arnold adjusted it. Made sure it covered her front, as she was still naked underneath.

"They are my wings," she whispered.

"What did you say?" Arnold asked, as he didn't think he had heard it right.

"My wings," she repeated and pointed towards her back. "He said he wanted to give me wings, that all angels should have wings."

"And you were his angel?" She nodded and looked down. "The others here, are they angels too?"

"No." She was shaking and started crying. "He says I am the only one who can fly."

"Fly?" Arnold asked, and she nodded again. "What do you mean?"

"From the building. Me and Jasper, we wanted to jump. But I was the only one who jumped. Jasper was too scared."

"Who is Jasper? Is he the one who did this?"

"No, he is my friend. He saved me. I jumped, and he saved me. I landed in the trash, and he helped me get out. He is my friend. He is almost eleven years old. He helped me get better. Told me, I was a real angel."

"Is he here now?" She shook her head. "Did something happen to him?" She looked down. "Did he get hurt? Did that man hurt him? Linda, did that man hurt him?" She nodded, and tears fell down her cheeks. "Okay, come with me. We better find you some clothes and maybe get you some food, yeah?"

"Others?" she asked and looked at the basement.

"Don't worry; we'll take good care of the others."

"Buch," his female colleague called him over to look at the scarring on the girl's back. He gave Linda's hands a little squeeze and stood up. He didn't think that anything could startle him anymore. That was, until he saw the girl's back. All air left his lungs, and he felt as though a blade was cutting down his own back.

Deep scars covered her skin. There were many cuts, too many to count. They had been cut in a pattern. Small cuts, long cuts, deep ones, and superficial ones. It was like a painting, like someone had carved out a set of wings on the little girl's back. He could only see the top of half, but he guessed they went all the way down her lower back. How was she supposed to forget when she had a constant reminder like this? How was this little girl ever going to be alright?

He wondered how it had happened and shivered at the thought of the pain she must have gone through.

"Buch?" A voice called at him, but he just kept staring at the scarring. "Buch?"

"Buch?" Jensen's voice cut through, and Arnold looked up. "Are you okay? You have been staring at the ground. Do you need a minute?"

Arnold shook his head and got up from the chair.

"No, I am okay, thank you." He walked over to Trish and took her hand. Though she was dead, he didn't want her to feel alone.

"Should we get going then?" Iversen asked, and Jensen made a move to leave.

"Just a minute." Arnold interrupted and turned to Dijana. "There is a thought I cannot let go of. It is probably nothing, but I need to ask." He took a deep breath and shook the image of the scars out of his mind. "Does she have any scarring?"

"Scarring? Do you mean the stab wound or what?" Dijana asked, looking over the files.

"No, not that. Something not meant to kill her. Something superficial, like on her back and shoulders? Does she have anything like that?"

Dijana swallowed and took a step back.

"Why do you ask?" Her voice was shaky, and Arnold got a bad feeling.

"She does, doesn't she? Do they look like wings?"

Dijana's eyes widened, and she looked through some files, found a stack of photos, and handed them to him.

"Wings," he whispered and felt the stabbing pain in his chest again.

"How did you know?" she asked.

Jensen and Iversen also stepped closer to have a look at the photos.

"Cause I have seen this before," Arnold said and held one of the photos into the light. The photo showed a woman's back. Deep cuts covered it in a pattern to look like wings. Just like he had seen on Linda those many years ago. "Do they all have these?" he asked.

"Trish doesn't, but the rest of them do. At least the ones I've been able to look at."

"Trish does not?" Dijana shook her head. "In other words, everything is different about Trish. She is older than the rest, a lot older. She is the only one stabbed. She is blonde, though that might just be colouring. She is the only one buried alive and the only one without wings. Why is she different? Why didn't he murder her like the rest?" The others didn't answer. He wasn't really talking to them; it was another one of his coping mechanisms, a way for him to process information and think. "Is it possible the others were drowned?"

"Yes, that is very possible. It will be difficult to determine conclusively, but it is definitely a possibility."

Arnold swallowed. He was back. *How can he be back?*

CHAPTER 10

A small hand pressed on Linda's back, rubbing gentle circles, and she glanced over. Tucker had been so strong through it all. It scared her how little he was affected by it. She suspected that maybe he didn't understand; maybe he didn't realise what he was doing when he shot and killed his own father. She hoped he would forget it, that his brain would protect him from this memory. She knew first-hand that it was possible. As a kid, she had been through so much, but now as an adult, she could hardly remember any of it. *He will be fine, right? He will be okay.*

He crawled into her lap, and she hugged him closer.

They would be okay. They had to be.

The train made a stop, and more people got on. The seats slowly started to fill, and Tucker clung to Linda, held on tighter and tighter. He was tired; he hadn't slept at all since leaving the house. Linda hadn't slept, either. It wasn't till now she felt sleep pulling her in. Her eyelids got heavy, and once she felt Tucker's slow breaths against her chest, she too gave in. Her head rested heavy against the window, slowly bouncing as the train moved.

Sounds of laughter in the train startled her from her sleep. A family in the nearby seats were playing a card game, and the youngest was claiming victory. He was standing on the seats, cheering, with his arm above his head. His older brother was laughing and cheering him on, while their parents apologised to the people around them and tried to get them to calm down.

Linda looked at her watch. They had been asleep for almost an hour. There were still many more hours to go before they were home. *Home*, she thought; *what a funny word*. She didn't know what that meant anymore. She had been sent on this assignment over three years ago. It was only supposed to have been for a couple of months. Ask around in the area, get some intel. The easy task had quickly proven to be difficult. No one wanted to say anything; no one wanted to get in trouble. After about six months, she had finally managed to get inside. Nate had shown an interest in her, and she had been hired as Tucker's nanny and caregiver. Of course, that job had quickly turned into much more than she signed up for.

Nate had raped her on her first night there, made sure she knew who was in charge and understood that he owned her now. If she disobeyed him, she would be handed to the others and sold off as property like the rest.

It had been a long time before she had managed to get word back to her boss. She wanted out. She hadn't signed up for this. But her boss had insisted. He had put the mission before her life, and by the time he had been replaced, it was too late. She had been in too deep and could no longer just leave Tucker behind. She'd had to see it through, had to keep fighting. So that was what she had done: fought.

She never thought they would have been able to escape like they did. Nate was dead, and they just walked out of there.

She had gotten more and more privileges over the years, and she and Tucker had been allowed to leave for shopping trips and park play time when granted permission, though Nate was often with them or had them shadowed. She suspected that with him dead, no one had given notice of them leaving. They were far away now, farther than they had ever been, but she was still nervous. She still worried that they would get caught and brought back. Or worse, that this was all a dream, and when she woke, they would be back in the same nightmare all over again.

Tucker was still asleep in her lap. His hands still gripped her jacket tightly. She stroked his hair. He needed a haircut. The curls twisted together and covered his forehead and eyes, made it difficult for him to see. If she gathered his hair, she could almost make a ponytail.

She would book an appointment for him once things had settled down. Once they were home. *Home*, she thought again. She wasn't even sure if she would get to keep him. Legally, she had no right. She was not his parent or his legal guardian. She knew, he most likely would go into the system, and they would have to part ways. She could try to get custody, argue that she was the only safe place he had. They would probably counterargue that because of their past history, she was the least suited person to take care of him. It could take years.

Maybe they were right. Maybe she was not fit to be a mother. Maybe the universe had known it all along, and that was why Willa had been taken so soon.

She wiped away a tear and rested her head back against the window. She couldn't afford to think like that. What happened to Willa was tragic and heartbreaking, but no one was at fault. It was just a terrible accident. Linda's only comfort was that her little girl had a wonderful life, however short it had been. She had been such an amazing little girl. Always smiling, always laughing. *God, I miss her.* She wiped away a few more tears and looked down at Tucker. *I will make sure you are safe, whether that is with me or someone else. I will make sure you are safe.* She wasn't certain if she was making the promise for him or for herself. Probably for them both.

Her stomach growled, and she awoke once more. This time, she was groggier, and her body felt heavy. Her neck was stiff, and she felt her spine crack once she moved a little. The relief made her smile a little, and she finally opened her eyes to look around. It was dark outside. She saw the lights shoot by as the train moved along, and though she didn't recognise anything, it still felt familiar to her.

The train slowed down and made a stop at the next station. She recognised the name and smiled. *I am home; I am almost home.*

She felt her stomach growl again, and she carefully shook Tucker awake.

"Sweetheart, it is time to wake up." Her voice was gentle as she cradled his face and kissed his cheek. "We are almost there. A few more stops and then we have to get off." Tucker lifted his head and stretched his arms above his head followed by a big yawn.

"Mom, I'm hungry." His voice was hoarse, and he yawned one more time.

"I know sweetheart; me too. Let's get some burgers once we get home, yeah?"

Tucker nodded with a big smile and leaned against the window to look out. Linda smiled as she studied the young boy. From looking at him, you wouldn't know what he had been through. Such a beautiful face with joyful eyes.

Linda moved her legs slowly, and Tucker started giggling, bounced up and down on her knees as he looked out the window and watched the lights fly by.

The train slowed down, and the next station was announced on the speaker. *We are here*, Linda thought to herself and helped Tucker put on his jacket. He waited patiently in the aisle as Linda put on hers and helped him with his backpack. It was a Spiderman bag. She had bought it for him last year. He was supposed to have started school, but of course Nate wouldn't let him. Said it wouldn't hurt the boy to wait a few more years. Linda had disagreed. Starting school was an important step in a child's life. Taking that away from him was like taking away a part of his life. Linda knew that first-hand, for she had lost that part of herself.

She had been so excited to start school, to finally learn something, just like her older siblings before her. She was born in February and therefore had to wait till after summer to start school. She had begged her parents to enrol her the year before, but they had thought it best to wait. When the summer break finally came, she had been overjoyed, and her smile had probably never been bigger than it was the day they went shopping for her first school bag. She had been with her father that day. He had taken some time off from the office to spend the day with his little girl.

He had stepped away for a minute to take a phone call while Linda was trying out bags. Just one minute. One minute was all it took for their whole lives to change. He had just walked around the shop, always within eyesight while he was talking on the phone. Something his colleague had said had annoyed him, and he had turned around to hide his frustration and end the conversation. After that, he had taken a slow deep breath and plastered on a smile as he had turned to continue the day with his daughter.

One minute. He had turned around for one minute, and she was gone.

The school bag his little girl had been holding just seconds before was laying on the floor, and she was nowhere to be found. She was gone. Taken away, and she never got to start school that year.

I promise you, you will get to start school, Linda thought to herself as she and Tucker disembarked the train.

Tucker talked the whole way, as they walked from the train station. Linda tried to listen, she really tried, but the reality had started to get to her. Here she was, walking in the streets of the town she once called home. Down the alley she knew so well. Towards the house she used to live in. Everything looked the same, the graffiti on the walls, the streetlight that flickered, even the rubbish containers were parked in the same spot. It was like no time had passed at all.

They turned a corner and passed the old bakery. A sweet scent of freshly baked bread made her smile, and Tucker's stomach started growling. They both giggled and continued walking. Grabbed some takeaway at McDonalds and continued through the town park. Made a left at the dam and walked up the hill, following a long narrow road through the forest.

"What is that?" Tucker asked and pointed towards the house at the end. Linda gave his hand a gentle squeeze and smiled at him as they approached the house.

"This is our new home." The teary sound of her voice surprised her, as she had not noticed she had been crying while walking through the woods. *I am home. I am finally home.*

CHAPTER 11

A knock on the door sounded early the next morning. Linda wasn't surprised. Last night, before going to bed, she had picked up her phone and called her handler, explained the situation to him. He had been worried; they had made a move on the operation that very same night and found Nate shot and the house empty. Everyone had been arrested, everyone but Gregg and a few of his top men. Linda wondered if that was why they hadn't been followed; maybe they had all been too busy escaping. But how did they know? Had they known she was a police officer? And if they knew, would they take revenge? Would they come for Tucker?

The questions had haunted her all night. She hadn't managed to sleep for more than a few hours, worried that someone would come and take Tucker away from her.

Tucker seemed more relaxed than ever before. After dinner, he curled up on the couch with his head resting in Linda's lap and his arms wrapped around her like a baby monkey. Linda carried him to bed but hadn't been able to untangle herself from him and instead ended curled up in the bed next to him. He slept the whole night. No nightmares, no mumbling in his sleep. Linda worried for him. Worried that one day, reality would hit him, and he would remember it all. His nightmares would return, and they would haunt him constantly, and not just in his sleep.

"Mommy, the police are here," Tucker shouted from the front door with a big grin on his face. He had never seen a real police officer before, let alone a police car; this was like his dream come true. "Mommy," he shouted again and ran through the house into the kitchen.

Linda laughed at the sight of him and held him close, as he jumped in her arms. "They have a police car," he whispered, and she swore she could see his eyes sparkle.

"Do they really?" Linda asked to play along. Tucker nodded enthusiastically.

"Hello, can we come in?"

"Can they, Mommy, can they?" Linda smiled at the boy. "Please? Please, please, please."

She nodded with a laugh and lifted him down as he ran back towards the front door. "You can come in," he shouted and ran back to Linda, looking over his shoulders to see the officers following him.

As exciting as it was to have real police officers within arm's reach, it also seemed a little overwhelming. Tucker hid behind Linda's legs and gripped tightly onto the fabric of her pockets.

After a few minutes of talking and pleasantries, they got up to go. Linda turned to Tucker with a smile on her face, excited to see the boy's reaction to what was about to happen.

"Sweetheart, do you want to ride in a police car?" The boy's eyes widened as he took in the question. The ecstatic glow on his face answered the question way before he blurted out a soft yes.

Linda's smile was just as wide during the car ride. Seeing the joyful face on that little boy made her heart sing. He was safe now, whether he was going to be with her or some other loving family. He was safe. That was all that mattered.

Tucker got the full tour of the police station, while Linda talked with her superiors. She knew she was in trouble. She had not kept in contract like she should, she had left without a word, and she had essentially kidnapped a child. Not to mention the shooting of Nate; she also needed to explain that.

The talk went on for over an hour; accusations were thrown at her, and she quickly got a feeling that she would be used a scapegoat to cover their own asses. The mission had not been the success they had hoped, and Gregg was still out there somewhere. She had risked her life, and with him on the loose, her life was still at risk, and they dared to blame her for their failures? She felt her fists tighten, and she snapped.

"With all due respect, sir, but I cannot see how this is any of my fault." Her voice was a lot louder than she had anticipated, but it shut them up, so she kept going. "I was chosen specifically for this task because you all knew from experience that I wouldn't crack under pressure. You chose me; you did," she spat, almost burning a hole with her eyes. "Not once did you send me backup; not once did you offer me an out. Not once. I was thrown in the deep end and expected to bring you information every week about the operation. Tell me, have I ever missed a delivery, huh? Have I ever not succeeded in giving you valuable information?"

"N-no, no, you haven't—"

"Exactly. I have delivered every time. For three years, I have given you information on a weekly basis, and yeah, I haven't managed to keep in touch over the phone, but guess what? Every time I asked to use a phone or was caught with a phone, I got punished."

She took a deep breath. Tears and snot were streaming down her face as she kept yelling and shaking more and more with every word.

"Do you want to know what that punishment was? Do you? I don't think you do, but I am going to tell you anyway. I was raped. And not just once, not just twice. I lost count how many times and how many men had a go at it. That kept happening till Nate took me in, announced me as his property, his slave to punish and abuse as he wished to do so. While all that was happening, I kept delivering want you needed, and I kept that little boy out there safe. I did all of that; I did. So don't come blaming me for your cockup, sir. If they sensed that someone was onto them, if someone tipped them off, then it wasn't me."

She folded her arms over her chest and tried to calm herself. Wiped her face on her sleeve and released her fists, feeling the burn from where her nails had been digging into her palms.

"I am sorry. You are right. There was a mole within our ranks, but it wasn't you. We know that for certain. I didn't mean for it to sound like we were accusing you of anything. If it hadn't been for you, we wouldn't have been able to save as many people as we did. Thanks to you, we did not just shut down this operation but numerous others around the world. I know what you sacrificed for this, and I want you to know how grateful we are for your service." She nodded as a thank you but kept the firm stare at her boss. "Nevertheless, I am afraid we will have to put you into protective custody." He held up his hand and continued before she could interrupt him. "It is only for the time being. Besides, your old unit needs your assistance on a case."

"What case? I haven't worked on a murder case in years; what could they possibly need me for?"

"That is not for me to say. Buch and Iversen are on their way to your safehouse as we speak. They will give you the details. For now, I need to ask for your badge and gun."

"What?"

"You will be a civilian while you are under protective custody."

"No."

"Linda, please don't make this any harder than it has to be."

She felt her jaw tighten, and she was afraid her teeth would break under the pressure.

"What about Tucker?"

"We have been in touch with social services, and we agree that for the time being, it is best if he stays with you." Relief washed over her face. "Just for the remainder of the protective custody. After that, we will have to speak with social services again. He has clearly formed a bond with you, and if you play your cards right, it might be in your favour. But that means you will have to cooperate with us, and first step in doing so is handing in your badge and your gun. And before you ask, Buch and Iversen are aware. You will be assigned to their case as a consultant."

Linda nodded sighed before standing up.

"My gun and badge are downstairs; I left them here once I went undercover."

Her boss nodded and gestured to one of her colleagues behind her, and a box was placed on the desk in front of her.

"I figured as much. Therefore, I asked Wilson here to empty your locker. You will find all your personal belonging in this box. I just need you to sign these papers, and then you will have two agents assigned to you as protection."

"This way please, Miss Hemmer."

"Where are we going, Mommy?" Linda lifted the boy into her arms and gave him a kiss on the cheek.

"I am not sure, sweetheart, but all that matters is that you and I are together, right?" Tucker nodded with a smile and hugged her, hiding his face in the crook of her neck.

"We do not think your identity has been leaked, but we cannot be sure. So for the time being, you will be set up in an apartment with twenty-four-hour protection. We must ask that you do not leave the apartment at any time, unless it is preapproved, and you will be accompanied by two agents at all times." Linda scoffed a laugh and rolled her eyes. *What was the point in escaping then?* she asked herself but pushed the frustrations away. Choose to focus on Tucker and keeping him safe. Everything else could wait.

The little boy fell asleep in her arms again, and she hugged him closer. She thought of her family and how they would help her love this kid. She smiled slightly, knew that her sisters would be overjoyed to have him join their family. Trish had long talked about what a terrific mother Linda was and how she wished for Linda that she would find the strength to try again. To have another child. *Some people are meant to be parents, and some are not*, Trish had said, *and you, Linda, you are meant to be a mother.* Back then, Linda had been offended and hurt at the statement. Hurt, because she already was a mother, and she always would be. Of course, that was not what Trish had meant, and Linda knew that. The moment she and Andrea had Willa, they were both parents. Losing her in a tragic accident did not make them any less. They would always be her parents, and she would always be their precious daughter.

Linda looked at Tucker again when the car made a stop. He was still fully asleep, and she had to carry him inside once the area had been cleared. Giving the apartment a onceover, she was happy they both had managed to shower at her place before going to the station. This place did not seem to have electricity, let alone running water.

"This is just a temporary place. We are trying to make your house safe enough, so you can stay there with officers parked outside," one of the agents explained.

Linda just hummed in acceptance and tucked the boy in his bed, kissing him goodnight, before making her way to the living room area.

In there was none other than her old friend and saviour, Arnold Buch.

CHAPTER 12

Seeing someone familiar after everything they had been through sent a warm feeling of safety through Linda's body, and she couldn't help the smile that crept onto her face. Arnold soon reciprocated it and embraced her in a warm hug.

A sense of relief flowed through him at the knowledge that she was safe. "It is really good to see you."

Arnold's soothing voice made Linda smile even more, and she just tightened her hold around the older man, not caring what it looked like to everyone else. She needed this, and Arnold let her. He had always felt particularly protective over her, and when they started working together, she became a part of his family. He had been there to support Linda when she had returned from overseas. He had helped her make the switch from military to police and felt proud when she said she did that because he had inspired her. He had been there when she and Andrea had started dating. He had been there at their wedding, supporting Linda and walking her down the aisle when her own father refused to come. He had been there to welcome little Willa into the world, and when his own kids had been too busy during the holidays, Linda and her family of three had joined him and Annelise in their home to celebrate the holidays. He had been there through the tragedy that had taken Willa away all too soon. He had been there to pick up the pieces when Linda and Andrea's marriage had fallen apart, and now he wanted to be here for her again.

He wanted to help her through this, show her she was not alone in this world, there were people caring for her. She would need it; he knew she would.

"It is strange to see you again, old man, but it is good. It is really good." She smiled and briefly kissed his cheek. Arnold had been a father figure for her throughout most of her adult life, and she knew he would continue to be there through the rest.

"I agree." Arnold smiled and stepped aside to introduce Linda to his partner. "Linda, meet Iversen. He is going to take over for me once I retire."

Linda smiled and reached her hand out to greet Iversen. A shaky hand met hers while curious eyes looked her over and silence spread in the room. Arnold coughed to try and break the trance, but Iversen was completely consumed by the woman in front of him.

"Iversen," Arnold snapped, pushing his colleague gently on the shoulder.

Iversen shook his head and retracted his hand quickly.

"Sorry! Sorry, I didn't mean to stare, you just … You really do look a lot like her." The last part was said in almost a whisper, but not soft enough that Linda couldn't hear him.

"Look like who?" she asked and shifted her eyes between the two men in front of her.

"Your sister," Iversen said but quickly covered his mouth with his hands, seemingly just now realising what he had said.

"How do you know my sister?"

Iversen looked at Arnold and back to Linda, opening and closing his mouth like he was trying to come up with something to say. He had a weird look in his eye, and Linda got a bad feeling. She turned to Arnold with a questionable look and felt a knot in her stomach when he couldn't look her in the eye.

"You should probably sit down for this," Arnold said.

Every muscle in Linda's body tightened, and she felt all blood drain from her face. She knew that look; she knew it all too well. That was the look of guilt and sorrow. The look they all had when they went to tell family and loved ones about a loss. That look was never good. That look always meant a tragedy had happened.

"No," she whispered and slowly lowered herself onto a stool. She had seen that look before. Arnold had looked at her the same way before. "No." She started crying. "No!" Arnold didn't say anything, he just held her. Closed his eyes and let her fists beat against his chest as he pulled her close.

"I am sorry," he said quietly, and Linda sobbed against his shoulder. She was shaking and crying, and Arnold just held her close. Held her, like he had done years ago when he told her that Willa didn't make it. "I am sorry. I'm so sorry," he repeated and pulled her head against his shoulder. Her body had given up, and she collapsed completely. Her tense muscles all let go, and she unleashed a scream that cut through bones. Arnold had to hold her up and let her scream into his shoulder, as he just tightened his hold on her.

Everyone in the room stood paralysed. Lips trembling and eyes blank. No one said anything; they just stood there and let Linda's scream fill their souls.

Tucker had been forgotten in it all. He too was crying and shaking, though he didn't know what was going on. He didn't know why his mommy was crying, why she was screaming, or why the policeman was holding her.

Linda screamed again, and Tucker flinched from the sound of it. His mommy was hurting. She was crying. He had never seen her cry before. Never seen her break. She had always been gentle and smiled at him. She had always been strong and told him that they were okay.

He knew that his dad had been mean to her. He had seen them many times. He had been so angry at his dad, wanted to run to them and stop him, but Linda had looked unbothered and strong every time. She had never cried or screamed. So Tucker had decided to wait, had turned around and walked back to his room and hid under his bed. Linda was the strongest person he knew, and if she couldn't handle it, then no one could.

Every time his dad had hurt her, Tucker had hidden away and let it happen. *She will be okay*, he had told himself, and she always was. She always held her head high and she always had a warm smile ready for him when he returned from his hiding spot. She always smiled right after, like nothing had happened.

Now she was crying. She was screaming, and Tucker felt his heart tear open at the sound. His mommy was hurting, and he didn't understand why. The strongest person he knew had broken, and he just wanted to hug her, take away her pain and help her. Help her, like he had done when he had picked up the gun and fired it at his dad. He wouldn't think twice. Do anything for her. But this time, there was no one hurting her. There were no one he could save her from. Nothing he could do. There was just her. His mommy, and she was screaming, screaming like someone was pulling her heart out of her chest. Like she was feeling all the pain in the world, and as she felt it, Tucker felt it too.

It all became too much, and Tucker started screaming too. Fell to his knees and buried his face in his hands as he cried. Linda felt a hole in her chest and was pulled back to reality by the sound of her boy crying. She tightened her muscles again and freed herself from Arnold's tight hold. She half-crawled, half-pulled herself towards Tucker and wrapped her arms and legs around him, completely surrounding him with her presence and warmth.

She kissed his head and rubbed her hands down his back in slow, soothing strokes.

"It's okay," she whispered once she had found her voice again. "I am okay." She slowly rocked herself back and forth, rocking him with her. "I'm okay," she said again. "I am okay, you are okay, we are okay. We are safe." She tightened her hold around him and felt his sobs quiet down, as they slowly rocked back and forth. "I am okay, you are okay, we are okay. We are safe." She repeated it over and over. "We are okay. We are safe."

Tucker moved a little and put his arms around her neck, burying himself in her shoulder.

"Y-you okay, I'mmm- I am okay, we are safe," he whispered. Linda felt herself smiled with relief and kissed his head again.

They sat like that for a while. No one in the room moved. After, what seemed like hours, Linda felt Tucker's head fall heavy against her chest and his breathing evened out. He was sleeping. She wrapped his legs around her and lifted herself from the floor, with him clinging to her like a baby monkey. She walked to the bedroom and put him down on the bed. His little body seemed to get swallowed up in the big bed. She tucked the covers around him and sat on the edge for a bit before she kissed him goodnight and left him to sleep.

The others were waiting in the kitchen. Had made coffee and was sitting at the dining table. They didn't say anything, just looked at her as she sat down. Arnold handed her a cup of coffee and placed a comforting hand on her shoulder. It made her smile slightly, he always had a comforting touch.

"Okay, can we continue now?" Iversen asked. All eyes snapped to him, and he caught a sense of annoyance from them all. "What? It's not like we have all night."

"Iversen!" Arnold's voice was stern, but Linda cut him off.

"It's okay. He is right; you are here to talk to me about a case. I can grieve my sister later."

Her voice was calm, her tone even. Arnold looked down at the floor and took a breath. It shouldn't be shocking anymore when she did this. Yet it was. No one should be able to switch their emotions on and off like that. But she could. He had seen it so many times. It was how she coped with things. She became this cold, emotionless shell. All life seemed to vanish from her eyes, like she had put herself on pause. Autopiloting through. It was efficient; it was part of what made her such a great undercover agent. Though Arnold feared that she would get stuck in this state one day. That one day, it would all get too much, and she wouldn't be able to come back again.

He looked at her robot-like expression and wondered if it was just a matter of time before the switch would be permanent. He shook his head, couldn't finish that thought, feared that an emotionless Linda Hemmer could be damaging to them all.

He had seen people lose their humanity before. Seen them lose themselves, and it had cost a lot of lives. Cost a lot of tears and anguish. Looking at Linda now, he swore he would protect her from that. Create an environment where she could be human and switch her emotions on and keep them on. A safe space, where she wouldn't lose herself, lose her humanity.

CHAPTER 13

It had taken a lot of convincing and a lot of arguing, but Linda finally agreed to spend the week with her family. She had been through a lot, enough to drive anyone crazy. She deserved a break. She needed it, and her family needed her. Arnold hoped that her spending some time with her family would allow her to grieve. Be vulnerable and human instead of closing herself off. Getting her to help on this case had been a mistake. He could see that now. The threat to her life and to Tucker's had proven to be minimal, and they eased up on the patrolling and the protective custody.

Looking at the case, they had gotten a few leads but nothing solid. Nothing of real importance. So many women were dead. So many lives lost, and they were nowhere near catching whoever did this.

Arnold watched Linda and Tucker play in the garden with Trish's two boys. *She will be okay*, he thought. It felt good seeing her like this. She was a good mother to Tucker, and that boy seemed to adore her. Arnold hoped she would get to keep him, she would finally have something good and stable in her life. Both for her and for Tucker.

He turned to walk away and looked over his shoulder one last time. Taking a mental image for later.

Linda was laughing. She was grieving and hurt and would be for a long time, but she was laughing. She had people around her who cared for her. They all had each other. She would be okay.

Arnold released a shaky breath as he sat in his car, looked at his watch, and tried to calm his breath. He hadn't gotten much sleep the past week, and Annelise had been furious. One night, she had gone to the station and dragged him home. He had fallen asleep almost the second his head hit the pillow. Since then, she had been over him like a hawk, and he had given more and more responsibility to Iversen and the team. He was still involved in the case. Still spending long nights at the station, but having Linda come home had changed things for him. Seeing her break down like that had broken something in him, and he had wanted to spend more time with his family. Didn't want this to be yet another Christmas where he was working.

But time was ticking. It had been almost two weeks since the terrible discovery in the woods, and the more time passed, the closer they would get to the inevitable: another murder. Another woman killed by this psychopath. Arnold could not live with that knowledge. As much as he needed a break from it all, he couldn't. It was not possible for him to rest till this guy was captured.

And that was how he found himself on his way to the one person he had sworn to never speak with again. The man who had started all of this. He who had given Linda her wings and taken away her childhood: the Angel Maker, as the news had labelled him.

Sweat ran cold down his spine as he heard the chains rattle through the wall. Footsteps approached the door, and a frail old man stepped through.

His hands were chained to the table, and the officers stepped aside, allowing Arnold to get a full look at the man in front of him. He looked nothing like he had back then. His muscle tone was gone, his broad shoulders crumbled and collapsed like he had been carrying stones on his back all his life. His skin was pale, almost transparent, and his face was wrinkled and unrecognisable. He had a tremor in his left hand. *Parkinson's*, Arnold thought. He had seen it in his file somewhere. Twenty-seven years had passed, and the man sitting across from him looked nothing like the devil he once arrested. Had it not been for his piercing blue eyes, Arnold would not have believed it to be him. But those eyes were unforgettable. They had haunted him for many years. For a long time after the trial, all Arnold had seen in his nightmares were those soul-penetrating blue eyes.

"I have been watching the news and figured you would show up at some point."

When the man spoke, Arnold felt chills all over his body. Yes, this was most definitely the man who had abducted and tortured poor Linda, and God knows how many other children before her. Arnold felt an anger burning inside he hadn't felt in so long. The thought of someone new out there like this man was sickening.

"So why don't we cut the small talk and you tell me what you know?" Arnold asked and leaned back in his seat. He was terrified. Being in the presence of this monster made him tremble to his bones, but he couldn't show him that. He couldn't show any weakness or fear. He couldn't give this man the satisfaction.

"I am sorry to waste your trip." The old man smiled. "As I said twenty-seven years ago, I had nothing to do with it."

Arnold groaned. He had heard this story before. This man repeatedly spilled the same lies, thinking he would get away with it. Just once, just once it would be nice to hear him admit to the truth. Take ownership of his wrongdoings.

"Enough," Arnold muttered through his teeth. "I caught you. I saw you watching that little girl die. I saw you stand there with wet hands and clothes. You drowned her in that tub. You took that girl from her family and destroyed her life. You tortured her and raped her for weeks. Don't sit here and deny it. You did that, you!"

The man across from him showed no sign of remorse. The accusations didn't even seem to faze him. He just sat back slowly, comfortably, and folded his hands on the table.

"Those are all the things I've been accused of," he said. "Though only some of those things I have admitted to. The rest, I did not do." He leaned forward again, and his bright-blue eyes seemed even brighter as he leaned into the light. "I will say this again: It was not me. I am not the Angel Maker that they speak of. I did try to drown the girl, and I did keep her from her family, but I never raped her. I did not give her wings, nor have I ever called her an angel. That was not me."

He spoke very calmly and precisely, and it made Arnold's blood boil. Why would he not just admit it? Why did he still insist on this story? He had been convicted, found guilty in all charges, but through the whole thing, he had only ever admitted to attempted murder and kidnapping.

"Why lie? What are you getting from this?"

"I am not lying. I never have, not about this. I did not do it. Besides, you are here because it is happening again, right?" he asked, and Arnold swallowed hard. "In fact, examining the bodies you have found, you realise that it has been happening ever since. It never stopped. It is all right there in front of you. You caught me, focused all your energy on me. Got me convicted, but all this time, I was not the Angel Maker. I am not the Angel Maker. He is still out there. He is still killing. Still searching for his angel, and he will not stop till he finds her."

"What are you talking about? Who is he?" Arnold asked.

"He had her twenty-seven years ago. Linda Hemmer. A beautiful little girl. She and her father walked into my bar one day. They went to the back. Her father seemed to have some sort of meeting with another man. He placed her in a booth by herself. A young boy came up to her, showed her a stack of magic cards. He was immediately captivated by her." He unfolded his hands and took a breath. "She was laughing with him, thinking she had made a new friend. Little did she know she had met the devil himself." His eyes got dark, and he looked down at the table. "I knew he was like that, and I knew what would happen. It had happened before. He had been fascinated before, but I never imagined it would go as far as it did." His tremor had gotten worse, and droplets of water spilled as he held the glass to his mouth and took a drink.

"What happened?"

"I know it sounds strange that I as an adult was intimidated by a child, but you don't know what he was like. I watched him strangle a cat once. He looked straight at me as he snapped its neck. The counsellor who placed him with us had described him as a child in need of love and comfort. Someone fragile who needed stability. We took him in without a second thought.

"My wife felt sorry for him, wanted him to have a good life. Her love for him blinded her, and it blinded me too. I didn't see the monster he was till it was too late. He came to us after a terrible traumatic experience. Both of his parents had been killed, his little sister too. He had been kidnapped and raped, all at the hand of their neighbour, whom the police shot as they entered his home. He had been drunk and had his hunting rifle around his neck. The same hunting rifle used to shoot and kill the three people next door. The police found the boy in a closet, naked with a broken glass bottle up his anus. From there, the case had been straightforward. The neighbour's DNA and fingerprints were all over, and he was in possession of the murder weapon, not to mention he had kidnapped and raped a little boy.

"A terrible story. But a story, nonetheless.

"You see, the neighbour did not do it. He was a drunk, and he hadn't picked up his rifle in years. His DNA was all over the house because he had been allowed to use their shower that week, as his own was getting repaired. The boy had brought him a casserole one night at the request of his mother. He had found the neighbour drunk and passed out on the couch. So, he had gone exploring through the house. He had found the rifle; his dad had one similar and had had been showing him how to shoot cans in the backyard, so he knew how to load it. He took it with him and walked home. Didn't think twice before shooting his mother, and then his father, and his little sister.

"Then he walked back to the neighbour's house, thought about killing him too, but then realised that he would get into trouble for this. Eleven years old, a cold-blooded murderer. So he wiped the gun clean, like he had seen on TV, and placed it around the old man's neck. Walked back home, past his dead family, and took a shower. Grabbed some dirty clothes and walked back naked through the garden to the neighbour's house, where the old man was still passed out on the couch.

"Then he raped himself with an empty bottle till it broke, shattered. And he called the police crying, saying he was hiding in the closet and that the bad man had hurt him and his family."

"How do you know this?" Arnold asked, his face white as a sheet at this point.

"He told me, told us. My wife took an overdose of sleeping pills that night, heartbroken from what this boy had told us. I wanted to go to the police, but I had child pornography on my computer, and he knew it.

"So I didn't say anything. We continued living, and when he told me I was going to help him kidnap that girl, I just did it. I didn't ask questions; I just did it."

Arnold felt sick. His hands were clammy, and sweat had soaked through the back of his shirt.

"I know, I am not innocent in all of this, that is why I am here in prison. I did try to kill that girl. I did, and not because he told me to. In fact, his exact words were to not hurt her. He was obsessed. I was hoping that by killing her, I would end it. That his obsession would stop, that he would stop. But it didn't go that way. She didn't die. She lived, again. Proving to him again that she is the angel he thought her to be. Part of me hoped it was a one-off. That he had learned his lesson and not done anything like it again. And since I didn't hear anything on the news, I kept hoping. Till now." The man looked up and met Arnold's gaze as he spoke again. "I am not the Angel Maker. He is."

"Who is he?"

"He calls himself Jasper, after the cartoon *Jasper the Friendly Ghost*. But when he lived with us, his real name was Hugo Ingolf Cooper."

CHAPTER 14

On the second day of the New Year, Linda found herself sitting on the edge of her bed with a written speech in her hands. She had on a simple black pantsuit and black heels. Her hair was pulled back and collected in a loose bun, a few rough strands of hair curled their way down her neck. Her eyes were blank and mascara already running down her face. She took a few deep breaths to collect herself before she stood up and walked downstairs.

Arnold and Annelise were sitting in the living room with Tucker. They had given him an old train set for Christmas; it had been a lovely distraction for the little boy. They had promised to look after him today. It was tough for Linda to leave him with someone else, but she needed to do this on her own.

She kissed him goodbye and received two warm hugs from Arnold and Annelise when a car horn sounded from outside. Her brother had arrived. It was time. She looked at Tucker for a little bit longer, and when she knew he was safe, she left and went out to greet her brother at the car.

He had cried too, had red puffy eyes and a broken look on his face. It was going to be a long day.

They didn't say anything on their way to the church. Neither of them could find the words to start a conversation, so they let silence fill the space, only broken by the humming of the engine and the cars passing by. Even after they arrived and walked up to the church, they still hadn't said a word to each other. And no words were spoken when Linda reached for her brother's hand and led them inside. Helen was sitting up front, her eyes heavy and with a tissue tightly gripped in her hand. She didn't look at them as they sat down beside her, Linda on her left side and Paul on her right. Still, they said nothing. What could they say? What was left to say? Trish was dead. Their older sister had been murdered, and now they were at her funeral. It all seemed so surreal, like it was happening to someone else, and they were just there to witness it.

The choir started singing, and a sob ripped its way through Helen. Both Linda and Paul reached for her hands and scooted a little closer to her on the bench. Linda interlaced their fingers and squeezed hard; she felt her sister squeeze back, and neither of them loosened their grip. They needed to feel each other, needed to feel the pain and numbness to know this was real. Still, they didn't say a word. They didn't sing along. Didn't cry. They just sat there and looked out into nothing, waiting for the time to pass.

The priest made a gesture towards Linda, and she tugged on the piece of paper she still held in her hand. Darren had asked her if she could say a few words. He would have done it himself, but he didn't think he could. Looking over at him now, Linda could see why. He was broken, completely and utterly broken. Of course, he didn't let it show; he had on a tight expression and held his head high, his arms tightly wrapped around each of his boys. Linda felt her throat tighten at the sight. Her she was feeling sorry for herself for losing her sister, and there Darren was fighting with himself to keep it together, to be strong for his sons. Trish's sons.

Linda took a deep breath, stood up, and made her way past Trish's photo and up the little steps to where the priest stood. He gave her a little nod before he stepped away, and she was now standing alone in front of a church filled with people. She let her eyes run over the crowd; so many familiar faces and yet so many she had never seen before. Her eyes met Darren's, and he gave her an encouraging nod. She could see he even tried to smile, but it never quite showed. She gave him a smile in return, or as much of a smile as she could muster.

"Hello, everyone, thank you for coming here today." Her voice cracked slightly, and she had to clear her throat to continue. "Sorry, I just realise this is the first time I am speaking today. I haven't really known what to say, so I just kind of stayed quiet." She looked down at her speech and broke out into a sudden smile. Half-laugh, half-sob escaped her, and she met Darren's eyes again. "Trish would have told me to get my shit together." A few people laughed, and she quickly looked over at the priest. "Apologies; I am not allowed to swear, am I?" It wasn't a question, but the priest gave her a gentle look, and the slipup made more people giggle. "She would probably have told me off for that too. Not that she was any better herself. If anyone could rip a few bad words, it was definitely Trish."

Darren smiled and nodded, and a tiny smile crept its way onto Liam's face. Linda saw it on her nephew and wanted to do everything and anything to make it all a little easier for her nephews.

"Jason and Liam, you may not know this about your mom, but she was the one who taught me to swear." Jason looked up and met the look of his aunt. "It is no secret that I was the rebellious one. To those of you who don't know me, my name is Linda, and I am Trish's little sister. The youngest one out of four: Trish, Helen, Paul, and then myself, with quite the age gap, if I may add." She looked at her parents with a devious smile and added, "I don't think I was planned."

More laughter broke through the crowd.

Linda looked down at her speech again; she had sidetracked completely after *Hello*, and decided to hell with it, Trish had never been one for traditions, anyway.

"When I was asked to give this speech, I sat down and tried to find some stories to capture the essence of Trish. That proved to be a terrible idea, as I quickly had enough content to write a whole series. And the truth is, a few stories are not enough to capture all that Trish was, which is proven by all of you showing up here today. Trish touched the lives of so many people. So many. The church is full here, and we still have people standing outside on this January day, with snow falling and winds blowing, simply because Trish touched their lives in a way they wanted to be here today. I have been absolutely crushed knowing that my sister is gone, but looking out on all of you, I know the stories about my sister will never come to an end. Someone somewhere will always have something new to tell, or a different spin on an old story. By knowing that, I know her spirit will always be with us. Though she is gone, she will always be in our hearts. And the stories and memories we shared with her will be carried down through generations, because that is how important Trish was. That is the essence of her. The way she put a spell on you, on all of us. That is Trish. And that is a person I am immensely proud to have known. And I feel incredibly privileged to have been part of her life."

She looked down, wanting to lighten the mood a little again.

"Without Trish, I would probably never have learned how to tell someone to 'stick it where the sun doesn't shine' and be gracious while doing so." She winked at her nephews, and they sent her warm smiles. "I want to thank you all again for coming here today. And if okay with you, I would like to ask you one thing: let's not be afraid to talk about Trish, to share the stories and memories. It is healthy to be sad and to cry, but let's remember to laugh too. Trish had the best laughter, one that echoed through buildings, and she would have wanted us to keep smiling, keep laughing. So let's remember her, keep her essence, and she will always be with us. Thank you."

She stepped down and returned to her seat. Helen and Paul moved around and made a space for her between them, both needing to have her close after that.

The rest of the funeral went past in a blur. All of a sudden, they were out of the church, and everyone was shaking their hands and offering their condolences. Linda was saying, "Thank you," like a robot and not really registering who was standing in front of her or what they said. She just wanted this over with. She had been away from Tucker long enough now, and it made her worry. She knew he was safe with Arnold and Annelise; she just would prefer it if he was with her.

"Linda, my condolences."

She looked up at the man and recognised him as one of the police officers who had been with Arnold that day. *What was his name again?*

"What a great eulogy," he continued, still holding her hand in his own.

"Thank you." Linda smiled faintly and retracted her hand. She found it a bit weird of him to show up here, being the person who broke the news to her, that her sister had been murdered. *Iversen, I think his name is Iversen.* She let go of the thought and shook the hand of the next person in line.

This carried on forever, and she was getting frustrated by it all. Why couldn't they just leave them alone and go home? The service was over; there was nothing left to see. Suddenly, she was embraced in a warm hug. She was about to push away when a familiar feeling came over her. Her body reacted on its own, and her arms wrapped around the waist of the woman hugging her. A familiar perfume broke down her walls, and a sense of calm flooded over her. *Andrea.* It was all too much, and before she could stop it, she started sobbing into the woman's neck and the arms around her just tightened further.

Paul saw it and led the crowd away from them, wanting to give them a moment alone.

"Thank you," Linda whispered, saying those words genuinely for the first time today.

"No need for that." Andrea spoke and just kept hugging her. "I am here for anything you need."

Linda didn't say anything; she just stood there, accepting the comfort her ex-wife offered.

She would have stood there forever but felt like they were overstepping the line of what was appropriate, and Linda broke the hug, took a step back, and smiled at the familiar face in front of her.

"You look good," Linda said honestly and sent her ex-wife a warm smile.

Andrea just waved it off like it wasn't true, but it was. It looked like she hadn't aged a day. Like the divorce, the distance, the fallout, the loss, like it all had done nothing to Andrea. Linda caught a glimpse of herself in the window reflection but quickly looked away again. While Andrea looked untouched, Linda looked tired. She had lost so much weight and muscle tone, become ragged looking. Her hair had gotten matted and lifeless, and the bags under her eyes portrayed her state of mind and body. *I am so fucking tired*, she thought to herself. Tired of running, tired of missing what once was, tired of pretending like everything was fine, tired of losing people. Just tired of life.

"You do too," Andrea said with a soft smile. *Lies*, Linda thought but felt comfort in the words, nonetheless.

They stood there for a while, each of them looking at their feet, not knowing what to say. "I am sorry I wasn't here for your Gran's funeral. I only just heard about it. I am so sorry."

"That's okay; you are here now."

Andrea nodded and was about to say something more when a message pinged on her phone. She turned her face towards it. Linda hadn't meant to look. She didn't plan on it; it just kind of happened. *Madeleine* was the name flashing on the text: "Andy, honey, can't wait to see you tonight. I'll be wearing that … Linda didn't manage to read anymore before the screen was switched off and the phone flipped over in Andrea's hand again.

Linda felt her stomach turn like she was going to be sick. It didn't take a genius to figure out the rest. *She has moved on*, she thought. *Of course she has. Look at her; she is a frigging goddess.*

"How are …"

"I should …"

They spoke at the same time and shared a knowing look. Linda stepped into the woman's space again and gave her a brief hug. It was partly to say goodbye and partly to say thank you, but mostly it was because she just needed to have Andrea close just one last time.

"Thank you again," Linda said, squeezing her hand before walking towards her brother and sister.

CHAPTER 15

Linda was pulled from her sleep when her phone rang.

"Hello?" Her voice was groggy and hoarse from sleep. "Who?" she asked and shook her head a little to try and wake up. "Yes, this is she." The voice in the phone kept talking, and she had a feeling where this was going. "Send me the address; I will be right there." She hung up the phone and took a heavy breath. She had been here before; in fact, the situation was all too familiar.

She jumped slightly as arms sneaked around her, and she felt chapped lips against her neck.

"Who was that, babe?" the guy asked as he pulled her closer.

Linda grimaced, untangled herself from his arms, and made her way back to the bedroom. *Babe? Ah, well, maybe he doesn't remember my name, either*, she thought.

"Honey, who was it?"

Oh, no; you did not just call me honey.

"A bouncer somewhere," Linda explained vaguely. "An old friend of mine is drunk, and I have to go get her." She pulled a jumper over her head and buttoned her jeans.

"Do you want me to come with you?" he asked, already looking for his clothes.

"No. No, I will be fine."

"Are you sure, babe?"

Linda felt her body twitch uncomfortably again at the pet name, and she promised herself to never bring home a stray again.

"Yes. Yes, I am sure," she said firmly, picking up his clothes from the floor and tossing them his way. "But now that you are up, you can get dressed and make your way back home."

"What? Are you serious?"

"You're damn right I am serious," she muttered to herself and smacked the door after her. She sighed and then started the car, closed her eyes, and took a minute to calm herself before putting the car into gear and driving off.

What was wrong with guys lately? Normally, they would jump at the chance of a one-night stand. She had purposefully chosen dudes to keep her company for that very same reason, and she hadn't kept her intentions hidden. This was a one-time thing, nothing more, nothing less.

"Babe," she whispered to herself and felt her body twitch uncomfortably again. *We have known each other for four hours, and you start calling me "babe"? Fuck no. Ethan, Evan ... His name was something like that, right?*

She shook her head, turned on the radio. It had been a mistake to bring a guy home, but Tucker was staying the night with his uncle and cousins, and it had just felt lonely in the big house. She had thought about calling Iversen, but that would have been the furthest from a one-night stand as she could get. She couldn't do that to him. He was cute and sweet, but she wasn't ready for anything serious. If she was being completely honest with herself, then she was probably still in love with her ex-wife. That was just a whole can of worms that she was not ready to unpack yet.

She arrived at the bar and quickly recognised her friend Rick at the door.

"Thank you for coming. I sat her at a table at the back. We cut her off about an hour ago. I tried to get her to drink some coffee, but she just kept pushing me away and asking for you, shouting your name. She tried to call you, but as you can imagine, she couldn't figure out the whole hand-eye coordination, so I grabbed her phone and called you instead."

"Thank you," Linda said and walked inside. The place was packed, and it took her a few minutes to get through the crowd.

"Linda," someone shouted.

She turned to find Iversen standing behind her. "I thought that was you." He smiled and went in for a hug. Linda let it happen.

"Yeah, yeah, it's me. But what are you doing here? What is that?" she asked, pointing to the apron he was wearing.

"Oh, right; yes, this is my second uniform," Iversen answered, winking.

"Your uniform? You work here?"

"Yeah, my cousin owns the place, and I help out every now and then. I mostly do family gatherings and out-of-house services. You know, if you can't get to the bar, then we bring the bar to you. So what can I get you? On the house, of course."

"Oh, no. Thank you, but I am not staying. I am just here to pick up a friend of mine." Linda turned to point towards the back.

"Right, of course. I will let you get to it then. Let me know if you need a hand."

"Thank you." Linda gave him a quick smile and continued her way through the crowd. "Fuck," she mumbled to herself at the sight before her. "Hey," she said calmly and walked the last couple of feet. The woman snapped her head up at the sound of her voice, and a smile spread across her face.

"Liiiindaa," the woman cheered and went to hug her, but her legs gave in, and Linda had to catch her to prevent her from falling. *Oh, boy.* "You are here! My hero."

"Come on," Linda said and pulled the woman towards the front door. She felt the woman's lips brush the skin of her neck, and she had to curse internally and bite her tongue. Solidly past her tipping point.

"You are so warm," the woman said.

Linda ignored her and helped her into the car.

They didn't say anything during the ride. Her drunk companion had fallen asleep against the door. *Thank God,* Linda thought. She was too tired and angry for any sort of conversation at this point. Though she couldn't help herself but look over at the woman, a faint smile showing at the corner of her mouth.

She pulled into the driveway and got out of the car slowly, made her way to the other side, and gently shook the woman awake.

"Andrea," she called. "Andrea, wake up."

"Linda? What are you doing here?" Andrea asked and stretched in the car seat like a cat.

"I am bringing you home. Now, come on." Linda pulled her ex-wife out of the car and towards the apartment complex. Thankfully the main door was unlocked, and they could get inside.

The steps proved trickier, and she basically had to carry Andrea up the stairs.

"So strong," Andrea purred against her neck, and Linda felt goosebumps on her entire body.

"Stand here," Linda said and put her down when they reached the apartment door. She rifled through Andrea's purse to find the keys and didn't notice the woman leaning towards her.

"Hi," Andrea whispered and looked up at her. The little hight difference became noticeable from where Andrea stood without her heels on. "You smell different. Cologne."

Linda ignored her still and started looking through her ex-wife's pockets when she didn't find the keys in her purse.

"Since when do you wear cologne?"

"Andrea, where are your keys?"

"You slept with someone," Andrea blurted out and punched Linda on the shoulder.

"Ow! What was that for?"

"You slept with someone," she stated again. Linda met her eyes and she looked hurt. Why did she look hurt?

"Yes, I had sex. Happy now?" She turned her focus to the purse again and went through it systematically, checking every corner and pocket. "How can you always fit so much crap in here but not have a place for your keys?"

"Was he good?" Andrea asked, and Linda looked up.

"Who?" Linda asked.

"Your boyfriend."

"I don't have a boyfriend."

"So he was just a one-night stand, then?" Andrea leaned closer again, and Linda tried to concentrate on finding the keys. "Was he good?"

"I am not telling you."

"Why? Because I'm drunk?" Andrea asked, and Linda nodded. "I am drunk."

"That would be the understatement of the year," Linda said and helped Andrea to stand fully on her own. "Andrea, where did you put your keys?"

"I don't know." Andrea shrugged and fixed her stare on Linda's lips.

Linda craved to do the same but refrained and instead created some distance between them.

"Come on, you have to tell me. They have to be here somewhere." She heard something rattling at her fingertips. "Ah," she exclaimed and was about to pull the keys out when Andrea stopped her.

"You're still as beautiful as ever," Andrea stated, like it was all that Linda was hoping to hear. And when she blushed, Andrea thought that it was. "I love your hair like this, frizzy," she whispered and began to play with a strand of Linda's hair.

"No," Linda whispered and closed her eyes to not fall into this trap.

"I love you," Andrea said.

"What?"

"I love you," she said again.

"You can't just say that."

"Why not? It's the truth. I'm still so in love with you. It feels like I am living a lie now."

Linda didn't know what to say or do. She just stood there, eyes wide, her mouth open.

The lights turned on inside, and suddenly the door opened.

"I thought I heard something," came a bright voice.

Linda looked up and locked eyes with a young blonde woman. She was beautiful. *Madeleine*, Linda thought and felt her jaw tighten.

Madeleine fixed the rope around her body tightly and opened the door more for Andrea to come in. But Andrea took a step in the wrong direction, and Linda had to ignore the butterflies when Andrea wrapped her arms around her and nuzzled her face into the crook of her neck.

"So strong," Andrea mumbled again and started kissing the skin below her ear.

Linda tensed, untangled herself from her ex-wife, and handed her to the woman at the door.

"You must be Linda," the bright voice sounded again. It wasn't really a question, but Linda found herself nodding anyway. "I have heard everything about you. It is good to finally put a face to the name. I am Maddy."

Linda shook her hand and had to retract it fast when Andrea seemed to think it was her she was reaching for. "Thank you for bringing her home." *Home.* Linda's jaw tightened again, but she fixed a smile and held her head high.

"Of course." The door was closed before she could say anything else, and she was left alone in the hallway as the lights went out. *Terrific, just wonderful.*

Thankfully, her companion from before had left when Linda returned home. Though, she couldn't help but feel alone in the house now. She had never really spent any time there on her own.

After Willa's death, Linda blamed herself for the accident, and her self-hatred had become destructive. She had pushed away everything and everyone around her, and their marriage had quickly fallen apart. Looking back, Andrea had tolerated her for far longer than she had expected.

After that, Linda had thrown herself into her job and spent more time at the office than her home. Not long after, she had changed departments and had basically been on undercover operations since.

This was her first night alone in the house, and for the first time in a long time, she found herself longing for a glass of wine or something stronger to take away the loneliness.

CHAPTER 16

It had been a month since the funeral. Everything was still raw, and emotions were still running high, but there was also a sense of calm over the family. Closure in some way. The police had caught the Angel Maker, and he had confessed to every single murder, given details of it all that only the killer could have known.

They had caught him; now no one else had to die.

Arnold had started his retirement, finally having time to spend at home with his wife. Linda had laughed at the thought. There was no way the two of them would survive being around each other 24/7. She had been right. It had only taken about a week for Annalise to send her husband out of the house. Having him home was driving her crazy. He needed a hobby, and he needed one quickly.

Linda suggested he go fishing. The area around the town had several great fishing spots, and according to her, fishing was something that calmed the soul. She had given Arnold a fishing rod for Christmas and spent the last few weeks teaching him how to use it. Tucker had followed along and seemed to catch on much quicker than his Gramps; that was what he was calling Arnold now: Gramps. Annalise was Gran. It had caused some tension in the family, as he was still referring to Linda's parents by their first names, whereas her brother and sister were now Tucker's aunt and uncle, and all of Linda's nieces and nephews were his cousins. It made Linda smile. Tucker had a family now, a real one, and they all loved and cared for him.

He was safe. For the first time in his life, he was safe.

Linda had started the adoption approval process. She wanted Tucker to be hers, officially, and they were not far from that goal now.

She had never imagined that this was what her family would be, but she was grateful.

One day, Tucker asked about Willa's room, and Linda showed him. They looked at pictures of her little girl, and Linda told him stories of Willa. She hadn't told him directly that Willa had died, but Tucker seemed to understand it anyway. "She can help take care of Aunty Trish now," he had said, and his words had given Linda more comfort than she ever could have imagined. This little boy truly was something special.

Linda stood in the kitchen and slowly sipped her morning coffee. It was Monday, she was starting her new job today, and Tucker was starting school. He had been up an hour before the alarm clock and ran around the house in excitement. Thankfully, Iversen had showed up. He had promised to drive them, as Linda still didn't have a car. The accident from years back was still rooted deeply her, and she doubted she'd ever be able to drive again. It had been a challenge in the beginning just getting into the passenger seat of a car.

She looked out the window and saw Tucker and Iversen toss a ball back and forth. She smiled. Iversen had been a tremendous help through the past few weeks. She didn't even know him all that well, and he was just there if she needed it. It felt nice to have someone there, a friend she could rely on, someone who wasn't family. She knew he had a crush on her. It had become blatantly obvious after he had tried to kiss her a few days ago, but it was still way too soon for her to start anything with anyone. There were just way too many conflicting things and emotions that still needed unpacking before she could even think about going there.

Then again, he was cute. He was kind and caring, which was much more than she had been used to for the past few years, and he felt safe. He reminded her of a friend she used to have but couldn't quite remember anymore, but it filled her with a sense of calm. So maybe she would just give in to it, see where it could take them. She shook the thoughts away and knocked on the window, signalling for the boys that it was time to go.

They arrived at Tucker's school, and the boy's face was as bright as the sun.

"I will have so many friends," he exclaimed as he kissed his mommy and ran off towards his teacher.

"He will be fine," Iversen said at the look of worry on Linda's face.

"I know, but what about me?"

Iversen chuckled and started the car.

"You will be fine too," he said, and they drove off.

Minutes later, they arrived at the office building in the city centre. The building was smaller than she had remembered, though still five stories tall and with the same impressive building structure. "Do you need me to pick you up after work?" Iversen asked.

Linda turned to him and said, "No, no, it will be fine. I have a short day today, so I will take the bus to go pick up Tucker, and then we are having dinner with Arnold and Annelise."

Iversen nodded and gave her a smile before he drove off. Linda took a deep breath and walked into the building.

Everything looked the same as always, even the receptionist was still the same person. "Good morning, Miss Olsen," Linda greeted the woman at the reception desk, who rolled her eyes and began to object, "You know I hate to be called …" She lost her train of thought as she looked up and recognised the woman standing in front of her. "Linda," she exclaimed, jumping out of her seat. "They told me you had come home, but I couldn't believe it!" She quickly rounded the table, said, "To hell with personal space," and immersed Linda in a hug. "Welcome home, darling." She smiled and was back in her seat just as quickly as she had gotten out.

"Thank you, Vivian. It feels good to be back."

"Well, it is fantastic to have you. Now, make sure to stop by me before you leave today, and I will have your badge ready for you. For now, if you could please sign in here." She pushed a tablet towards her, and Linda signed her name. "I believe you know your way?"

Linda nodded and wished her a good day.

She was back. She was actually back, and it felt good. She had missed this.

The elevator doors opened, and she stepped through. A smile spread on her lips as a memory found its way to her from her first time in this exact elevator. This was where she had met her wife.

"Oh hi, you must be Miss Williams." Andrea had almost jumped at the sound and snapped her eyes up from her phone. No one ever spoke to her; no one ever dared. She was met by a pair of soft blue eyes and a smile bright and honest. *Say something*, she thought to herself.

"Eh, uh, yeah, yeah. Yes." She swallowed and mentally kicked herself. *Great job, Andrea, very smooth.* She tore her eyes away and looked back at her phone, expecting the woman to be regretting making contact after that encounter. But much to her surprise, she saw a hand move towards her and the soft but rusty voice sounded again.

"Nice to meet you, I'm Linda."

Andrea stood paralysed for a second before she shook the woman's hand and was met with another bright beaming smile. She felt herself smile back, completely entranced. What was this sorcery? She never smiled, not at work. Not at all, in fact.

Linda continued talking, waved her hands around like she was telling a story. It was probably a good story, anything with that rusty voice would be enticing. But Andrea couldn't bring herself to listen. She was too distracted by the way Linda's t-shirt hugged her body tightly, tugged into the waistband of her jeans. The short sleeves under pressure as her arms flexed with every movement. *Stop it, Andrea!*

Andrea shook her head and met Linda's eyes again. So blue.

Quit looking into her eyes like that.

She blinked a few times and tried to focus on something else. That's when she noticed the deep scar across the woman's eye. The imperfection somehow made her even more attractive. She tore her eyes away, and Linda spoke again.

"It was lovely meeting you." Her smile beamed bright at Andrea again before she made her way out of the elevator, and Andrea tilted her head watching her.

"Yeah. Yeah, great meeting you too," she whispered to herself as the elevator doors closed.

Andrea had told her the story at their wedding. Linda had at the time been completely oblivious to the effect she had had on her boss. But the nonstop flirting and longing looks had caught her up in the end. Very much against work policy, but since Andrea wasn't directly her boss, there wasn't much HR could say about it. It also quickly became apparent to anyone interacting with the two of them that this was not just a fling. This was real. Of course, it had been a running joke in the department that soft little Linda Hemmer had managed to turn the stone-cold Ice Queen into a puddle with just her smile.

Linda chuckled to herself and prepared to exit the elevator when suddenly Andrea stood in front of her.

"Hi, hi," Andrea stammered, and Linda chuckled again at the similarities to their first encounter.

"Hello, Andrea; it is good to see you again." She smiled and nodded politely towards her ex-wife before she stepped out the elevator and walked past her.

"You're back?" Andrea asked, still shocked to see her.

"I am back, yes."

"Right, of course you are; you are here." Andrea smiled. "How are you?" she asked but stopped herself. "Sorry, that was a stupid question. Don't answer that. Just … let me know if I can do anything, please?"

Linda nodded and gave her a warm smile.

"Thank you, I appreciate it. And to answer your question, I am doing okay. Things are … tough, but they are getting better. Tucker started school today, so we are all very excited." Linda wished her a good day before she walked back to her desk.

"Yes, have a good day," Andrea whispered long after Linda had gone and stood lingering for a moment longer before finally stepping towards the doors, the elevator of course long gone, and she had to press the button again.

CHAPTER 17

It was an early Friday morning; Tucker was going on a trip with his school. He had been incredibly excited all week, and despite Linda's concerns, she was happy for him. This was what he was missing out on; this was what she had promised him once they escaped: for him to be free and make friends.

His first day of school had been, in his own words, the best day of his life. The other kids had already been halfway through the school year, so when he started, he was the new kid, and they all gathered around him like he was a shiny new toy. Everyone had shown an interest in being his friend; Tucker had never received that much attention and kindness. Slowly over the week, the interest in him seemed to fade, but Tucker hadn't been bothered. He had already picked his three best friends.

His first friend was Timothy; he was a quiet kid with glasses and a turtle. He had been bullied in school before Tucker had stood up for him and got in a fight with one of the older kids at school. All the other kids had stood up to him against the principal and told him what really happened. Tucker got off with a warning, and Linda had been called in to school to be lectured in how violence was never the answer. Normally, Linda would agree with him, just not in this case. She had calmly asked the principal what he would have done if someone twice his size had initiated the fight and punched him in the face. Would he just keep taking the punches and risk becoming this boy's punching bag, or would he get up and stand tall and show him that this was not the way to treat someone else?

Tucker had done the latter. He had fallen to the ground and gotten back up again. He had told the boy that he didn't want to fight him, that they could talk it out, just like Linda had taught him, but the boy had just laughed and launched for him once more. This time, Tucker had ducked and avoided the hit. He then warned the boy, told him that if he tried to hit him again, he would fight back. Again, the boy had laughed and launched a third attack. Tucker simply kicked him in the groin and then punched him in the chest, making the boy fall to the ground.

Afterwards, Tucker offered the boy a hand to get up, but that was when the teacher had broken them apart and sent them both to the principal's office.

Tucker had cried when he came home, told Linda he hadn't wanted to fight but that other boy just kept trying to punch him, even after all the warnings, so he just snapped and fought back. Linda had comforted him and told him he had done everything right. It was never okay to start a fight, but if there was no other way around it, then it was always okay to defend yourself. She didn't know if it had been the right thing to say, but it was what her father had told her when she had been a kid.

His second friend was Anna; she had been the one who stood up for him and told the principal the truth about the fight. She was a smart kid and could talk your ear off if you let her.

His third friend was Brett, the bully. That's right; Tucker had made friends with the boy who had punched him. Linda had been a bit wary of that friendship in the beginning, but Brett proved to be a good kid. He wasn't very smart, but he came from a similar background to Tucker, and they talked about that a lot. Linda figured it was good for them both.

It was an odd combo of friends, but they seemed to get along very nicely. Brett had apologised to both Tucker and Timothy, and Anna had invited him to join them on their quest to slay the dragon in the forest (the dragon being an old tree that had fallen over in a storm). Odd friends were oftentimes the best ones.

Linda kissed her son goodbye and watched the car drive off as another car approached. She recognised it straight away. *Iversen; what does he want?* They hadn't really spoken since the weird encounter at the bar last week. She had a feeling it was only a matter of time now before Iversen would ask her out, and she had been trying to come up with an answer. A polite way of saying no. He was a good guy, and she didn't want to lead him on, but she also didn't want to break his heart.

"Iversen, hey, what are you doing here?" She greeted her friend, smiling, 'cause that's what they were: friends. Nothing more, nothing less. *Oh, I really hope it can stay that way*, Linda thought and went inside, with Iversen following on her heels.

"Sorry for just showing up here unannounced, but I was hoping to take you out to dinner, since you are child-free this weekend and also because I just really want to take you out to dinner." He smiled. *Oh no, he is smiling. Why is he smiling? Does he think I will say yes?*

"Ah, look, Iversen," she started and avoided his eyes, but he cut her off before she got any further.

"If we are going to be dating, don't you think it's time you call me by my first name?"

Dating! What? No.

"Sorry, Iversen; I don't know your first name, but I also don't think—"

"It's Jasper, my first name is Jasper," he interrupted again.

"Okay, Jasper. I am really sorry, but I—" Linda tried but was cut off when he kissed her. She hadn't even realised how close he was standing, and now they were kissing. *No, no, no. I have to stop this.* She pushed him away and stepped around the kitchen counter to have space between them. "I can't do this."

"What do you mean?" He started walking after her, holding his hand to his heart. "Don't you feel the connection we have? Don't you know how long I have wanted this?" he asked.

Linda felt bad; she did know he had wanted it for a while, and it had taken her way too long to tell him no.

"I am sorry, Iversen." She used his surname on purpose, trying to emphasise that this was not happening. "I am sorry if I have been giving you mixed signals, but I am not interested." *Uh, that was a bit harsher than I had intended it to be. But he just kissed me. He didn't even ask for my permission.* When he didn't say anything, Linda decided to continue, making it clear that they were not happening. "I- I don't feel that way about you, Iversen. I am really sorry. You are a terrific guy, and I am sure there is someone out there for you. It's just, it's not me."

"It is because of her, isn't it?" he snapped and turned his back on her, like he was trying to calm himself.

"Because of who?" Linda couldn't help but ask.

"Andrea," he yelled as he turned back around. His eyes were dark, and the soft features were gone. Even his hair looked darker, like something had absorbed his kind soul.

"I think you should leave now." Linda spoke calmly but felt her heart hammering in her chest. She had never seen this side of him before, and she found herself afraid of her friend, scared of what he would do. "Leave now, please."

She spoke more firmly this time and kept her composure. The undercover operations had taught her this much, and she rarely ever flinched in situations like this.

Iversen took a few calming breaths but was still puffing like a wolf when he slammed the door shut, and Linda heard his car drive off moments later. *What the hell was that?* she thought to herself and found that her hands were shaking. She fumbled with her phone but managed to dial Arnold's number. Once dialled, she could hear his voice on the other end, but she couldn't get out a word of her own. Instead, she started crying and sank to the ground, thinking that the PTSD had taken over.

Arnold had been sitting in his chair with his feet up and a laptop resting on his legs. He and Annelise had been talking about going on a trip this spring. She had always wanted to see Paris, and now that he wasn't working anymore, they could finally do it. He was looking up flight details when his phone rang. A smile spread on his face at the sight of Linda's name on the display. It was always a pleasure talking with her, and he had just thought about calling to get her help with finding a good flight.

"Hey, Linda, good to hear from you. How did it go with sending Tucker off? Bet he was excited." He waited for her reply, but nothing ever came. "Linda?" He spoke again. "Linda, are you there?"

She had pocket-dialled him before, but for some reason, this felt different. He sat up in the chair and spoke her name again. That was when he heard the sniffles and crying on the other side. "Annelise," he called away from the phone, and his wife came into the living room.

"I would appreciate it if you would just come find me, instead of shouting for me because you are too lazy to get up," Annelise spoke and gave her husband a look. She quickly changed her posture when she saw the worry on his face, and he pointed to the phone.

"It's Linda; please talk with her while I go there. I will bring your phone with me."

Annelise nodded and accepted the phone.

"Linda, honey, this is Annelise. How are you doing, darling?" There was no reply, but she could hear Linda crying quietly. "Oh, darling, it is going to be okay. Arnold is on his way. He will be there shortly." She could hear more heavy sobs break out, and her heart clenched at the thought of sweet Linda hurting. "Honey, tell me, is your front door unlocked? I am not sure if Arnold got his key with him." She waited for a reply and heard a faint yes whispered in return. Relief flooded through her at the sound of Linda's voice. *She is okay.* "Okay, honey, where are you right now?"

"Kit- kitchen," Linda stuttered.

"Good, that is good, darling. Arnold should be there any minute now. Could you take a deep breath for me? Breathe in; one, two, three, four, five." She heard Linda take a breath in. "Hold it; six, seven, eight, nine, ten. And breathe out: eleven, twelve, thirteen, fourteen, fifteen. Hold it; sixteen, seventeen, eighteen, nineteen, twenty." She heard the breath release. "Okay, now once more. Breathe in …"

"I am here now, love," Arnold's voice sounded, and Annelise finally was able to release the breath she had been holding herself.

"Thank you, darling; please give me a call with an update, yeah?"

Arnold promised and hung up the phone.

"Linda, I am going to help you up now, okay?"

Linda nodded and felt Arnold's hands around her arms as he almost lifted her off the floor. "Can you stand, or should we sit?"

She pointed towards the chair, and he guided her around the kitchen counter till they sat at the dining table. He got her a glass of water and allowed her to compose herself before he spoke again.

"Do you want to talk about it?"

"Sorry, I didn't mean to disrupt your day."

Arnold put his hand on hers and made sure she was looking him in the eye as he spoke.

"Linda, never apologise for needing help. You are family, and there is nothing you can do or ask for that would disrupt our day. Okay?" She nodded, her eyes growing watery with gratitude. "Have you thought more about going to therapy? I know you weren't ready before, and that is okay, but maybe a few sessions wouldn't hurt. What do you think?"

"I think, I would like that actually." She sent him a warm smile.

CHAPTER 18

Francesca sipped her wine quietly on the couch, her eyes roaming over the pages of her book. She loved nights like these. Everyone else was sleeping, and a storm was glooming outside. All lights were out except for some candles and a reading light, just bright enough for her to see by its glow. She had a heavy blanket wrapped around her legs and the dog sleeping at her feet. It was perfect, nothing but perfect.

She looked at the clock and figured she should go to sleep after finishing this chapter. Thankfully, it was a long one, and she once again got consumed in the story. She almost forgot all about sleep and turned to the next chapter, when the dog lifted its head with a worried look and ears alert.

"It is just the storm, Buddy. It's okay; everything is fine." She calmed him and petted his head. "But we should get some sleep."

She reluctantly got up from the couch and put the book down. The dog followed her to the kitchen and watched as she put away the wine bottle and rinsed out her glass. "Do you need a pee before we go to bed?"

She looked at the dog, and his ears started moving again. She smiled at him and went to the porch door.

"Hurry up, I am just going to go brush my teeth, and then it is nighttime," she said and let the dog out. She went upstairs to the bathroom to get ready for bed. She was already in her pj's and just needed to wash her face and brush her teeth. Should give Buddy enough time to finish his business.

The porch door had been pushed open, and she could feel the wind picking up. It was going to be a stormy night. She chewed on her toothbrush and thought about securing the garden furniture but decided against it; she couldn't really be bothered.

"Buddy," she called and left the door open while she went back upstairs to rinse her mouth. "Buddy," she called, once downstairs and stepped out onto the porch. "Buddy! Buddy, come on, boy."

The wind picked up further, and she could hear the old oak tree creaking in the wind.

"Buddy," she called again, and then, she froze. That's when the rain hit. The sky opened up, suddenly and violently, and she got soaked within seconds. She squealed and rushed back inside. Thunder was booming in the distance, and she could see the sky light up behind the dark clouds. There was no way she was going outside to look for him now.

"Stupid dog," she mumbled, hoping he would see sense and find shelter in their garage for the night.

She closed the door and hugged herself, shaking from the cold. Her nightgown was dripping as she moved about inside; she began to dry herself before going to bed.

It all happened so fast. She had rid herself of the wet panties and was pulling her nightgown over her head when she suddenly felt a force push her to the ground, and her hands were tied with the gown above her head. She was about to scream when a wet cloth was stuffed into her mouth and something heavy weighed down on her back. *No,* she thought. *No, no, no! Stop it; stop it.*

She tried to fight it, tried to kick and scream, but it was too late. She felt the pressure and pain before she could do anything, and she found herself being raped violently against her bathroom floor. The man was rough. He pulled her hair and put an arm around her neck.

"This is your own fault, Linda," he whispered as the assault continued. "You rejected me, so now this is your punishment."

The woman cried and begged him to stop. She was not Linda. She didn't even know who this Linda was. She managed to spit out the cloth and felt her face being pushed against the tiles.

"Please," she begged. "I am not Linda; please." She was shaking and sobbing underneath her assailant. "Please, please just let me go. I won't tell anyone. I promise, just please, please let me go," she cried again, but the assault continued. And for every cry she let out, it got more and more violent.

"If I say that you are Linda, then you are Linda," the man hissed through his teeth.

His movements grew quiet, and he stood back up. She felt the weight of him easing, and relief washed over her.

"Mommy?" A quiet voice called from the hallway. *No!* Francesca thought and was about to scream for her child when the cloth was stuffed back in her mouth and this time tied in place with tape. Her hands were tied, and so were her legs. The man then smiled and lifted her off the ground.

"You have a child," he said with a grin. "What a nice surprise. Guess I have a long night in front of me." With that, he threw her in the bathtub and turned on the water.

Francesca screamed and kicked when he left her and went for the kid.

The water was cold as ice, and she shivered as she tried to manoeuvre her way out of the bath. Her arms were tied behind her back, and she tried to lift off while lifting her legs over the edge of the bathtub. She slipped, and her face hit the edge of the tub. She was bleeding now but tried again. Lifted her upper body with her hands and tried swinging her legs over. Her arms slipped, and she fell under water. Erratic splashing and kicking got her back up again. She could hear her daughter scream down the corridor, and tears welled up in her eyes.

She took a deep breath and let her upper body sink under while swinging her legs over the edge. She then pushed her arms back and half-crawled, half-balanced her way out of the tub. The greeting with the tiles underneath her was hard, and she hit her head again. Her vision was blurred, and she had trouble breathing with the soaked cloth in her mouth. She bit down hard and drank the water that got released. Did it again and again, until she finally got some breathing room.

She crawled to her front and got on her knees but kept falling over. All the while, her five-year-old daughter was screaming for her in the hallway. She cried and begged God for help.

But God never came. Help never came.

There was heavy breathing as the woman's lifeless body was tossed onto the bed next to her daughter's. The man cracked his neck and took a deep breath. He smiled as he saw the sight in front of him. The feeling he got when he drowned her in that tub was indescribable. The rush of energy that ran through him as he had snapped the little girl's neck. Oh, the pleasure of presenting the daughter's lifeless body to her mother. *That* had been the peak of it all. He had never done that before. As an adult, he had never attacked a child. But oh, did he enjoy it.

There was something special about taking the life of something so pure, so innocent. He had almost forgotten the sweet, sweet taste of taking a child's innocence away.

"This is your doing, Linda," he whispered as his eyes roamed over the two lifeless bodies in front of him. "You made it clear that you don't want me, so now I had to take it for myself. It is your fault. It is all your fault. I had sworn to never do it again. Don't you see? We found the killer; we found him. Well, it wasn't him, but he was a fan. He was willing to take the fall for me. Everything was good in the world again. But no, you just had to go and fuck it all up again. 'I don't feel that way about you, Iversen. I am really sorry.' Fuck you."

He slapped the dead woman and wrapped his hands around her neck.

"You are such a fucking bitch. You swore you would never leave me, that we would never leave each other. But you left. You fucking left me. Arnold fucking Buch came and took you away from me, and I have been looking for you every day since. Don't you see that we belong together?"

He released his grip and got off the bed.

"We belong together. And we will be together again. Just you wait and see. Once you have seen what I have done, you are going to come looking for me, and we can finally be together. You will never leave me again. I will make sure of it. Always, always shall we be together." He stroked the dead woman's cheek and kissed her softly. "My sweet angel."

CHAPTER 19

The room was small, and the ticking of the clock on the wall seemed to get louder each second. Linda looked at the counter as it ticked away, one second at a time. She heard the door open behind her, and an elderly man walked in. He had a white beard and a kind smile. Linda knew him from before. He had been her therapist in the past, and he was the only person she trusted to do this. She felt her hands stick together and figured she was sweating through her clothes. Her leg was jumpy, and she looked around the room. It felt like the walls were closing in on her, like there was no air to breathe.

She was asked to lay back and close her eyes. Take deep breaths and count down from ten.

"Imagine you are standing in a forest. All around you are trees, and in between those trees, you can see the sun shining. Start walking towards the sunlight. You find a path in the forest. Can you see the path?"

"Yes," Linda whispered.

"Choose a direction on the path and keep walking. You reach the end of the forest and step out onto a beach. Walk down to the water. Have you reached the water?"

"Yes."

"Touch the water. How does it feel?"

"Cold, it feels cold."

"Okay, you step out of the water and walk along the beach. Past the pier, you see a row of bathhouses. You walk over to the bathhouses. Are you there?"

"Yes."

"There are many bathhouses, and each one has a door. Each of these doors represents a memory from your past. Choose the memory that will take you back to when you were six years old. Have you found that door?"

"Yes."

"Open the door. What do you see when you walk through?"

"I, I see balloons. I think it is my birthday. It is my birthday. I am in bed, and my family is about to come sing for me. I have been awake for a long time, giggling while waiting for them."

"That is really good, Linda. Now, I want you to move forward in time a bit, a couple of months to a time where you are with your father; where are you now?"

"I am in my dad's office. I have a cold, and my babysitter is sick. He was supposed to be home and take care of me, but something happened at work. They called him on his phone, and he started yelling. He told me to get dressed and took me with him to the office. His secretary is nice. She is letting me paint on some paper."

"Good, Linda, good. Now, I want you to move forward a bit more, another couple of months. Find another time where you are with your father. Where are you now?"

"I haven't seen him in a long time. He is on a business trip."

"Okay, let's move a bit forward then. Another memory with your father. Where are you now?"

"I am in a bar. I don't think I am supposed to be here, but my dad has a meeting with a man. He tells me to sit down and be quiet. He goes to another table, and I am sitting by myself. There is another kid in the bar. He looks a bit older than me, maybe ten. He is smiling at me and makes a funny face. It makes me laugh. He comes over and shows me some cards. 'They are magic cards,' he says. He is really nice."

"That is good, Linda; now, where do you go after the bar?"

"We are going to look for a school bag. Dad promised me a new one. There is a blue one with red fire trucks that I really like. I want to show my dad, but he is on the phone. I try to call him over, but he just tells me to wait. I really like this bag, but I know it is expensive. I don't know numbers very well, but there are a lot of numbers on this one, so I don't think we can get it."

"Sounds like a nice bag. What happens next?"

"I see that boy from before. He is in the shop too. He says my bag is really cool and that he has one just like it. He is not using it anymore and asks if I want it. I just need to come with him, and then I can get it. I want to tell my dad first, but Jasper says we will be back before he finishes the phone call. So I go with him."

"Who is Jasper?"

"That's the boy. He says he is my friend."

"What happens then?"

"I- I don't know. It is dark and cold. I have been crying, and I have a headache. Jasper is there too. He tells me to be quiet, so the bad man won't come to find us. He helps me drink some water, and I feel dizzy. Jasper says we can get out, but we need to go on the roof. I don't think it is a good idea, but I do it anyway. I am really dizzy, and Jasper has to help me walk. We get to the roof, and he says we need to jump. I don't want to jump, but I jump anyway. It is like I didn't have a choice."

"What now?"

"I am not falling anymore. Everything hurts, and it smells funny. I think I have broken my arm. Jasper finds me and gives me a hug. He tells me that I am an angel, that he saw me fly like only an angel could."

"Do you think you are an angel?"

"I don't know, but Jasper says he will give me wings. He says all angels have wings."

"Do you have wings?"

"No, but when I wake up, it hurts on my back. Jasper says the bad man was there, that he hit me when I was sleeping and gave me wings. He shows me then in the mirror. I am bleeding. There is blood everywhere, and Jasper helps me wash it off. He says we need to wash it, so it doesn't get infected. It hurts, it hurts a lot, and I am crying. Jasper helps me drink some water and puts me to bed, tells me I am a real angel now. We promise each other that we will always be friends, that we will get home and always be together."

"What happens then?"

Linda shook her head violently and started moving on the couch. Her therapist put a calming hand on her arm and asked her to take a deep breath.

"I don't want to do this. The scary man is here, and he is going to hurt me."

"It is okay, Linda. It is going to be okay. Just keep breathing and tell me what happens."

Linda nodded and took a few deep breaths.

"He says, he is sorry. That he does not want to do this, but that he must. That it will not stop until I am dead." Linda started crying. "I don't want to die. I tell him, I don't want to die. I just wanna go home. He yells at me, tells me to be quiet, but I can't stop crying. He pushes me, and I hit my head on a table. It is bleeding, and it hurts. He keeps screaming at me to be quiet. Then he lifts me over his shoulder and carries me to the bathroom. He puts me in the bathtub. It is already filled with water. There is too much water in there, I can hear it falling on the floor. The water is cold, and I wanna get out. I try to get out, but he holds me down."

Linda gasped for air and dug her nails into the couch.

"What is happening, Linda?"

She kept choking on air, and her therapist told her to keep breathing, to stay calm and tell him what happened.

"I can't breathe. There is water everywhere. I can see his face above me through the water. He is holding me down. I try to come up for air, but he is holding me around my neck. I try to scratch him, but I don't have any strength left. I have to breathe. I have to breathe now." Linda choked on air again and started shaking on the couch, gripping for her throat.

"Thank you, Linda. You have done well. Now, I want you to go back in time to your six-year-old birthday. You are laying in bed, waiting for your family to come sing for you. Are you there now?"

Linda stopped choking, and her breaths calmed down.

"Yes."

"Good, now I want you to walk out of the door, out of the bathhouse and down to the beach. Are you there now?"

"Yes."

"Walk along the beach for me; follow your footsteps from before, and stop when you reach that spot by the water. Are you there now?"

"Yes."

"Touch the water, Linda; how does it feel?"

"It feels warm. The sun is shining more now; it is nice and warm."

"Very good, Linda. Now, leave the beach and walk into the forest. Find that path from before and follow it. Walk into the forest, through the dense trees, always with the sun in your back. Once you are done walking, open your eyes and come back to this time again. Whenever you are ready, just open your eyes."

Linda blinked a few times and took a deep breath. Tears flooded down her face, and she felt an overwhelming pressure on her chest. She sat back up and took a sip of water.

"What are you feeling right now?"

"I feel guilty. I just left with that boy. I left with him, even though I knew I wasn't supposed to. It feels like it was all my fault. That I somehow caused whatever happened to me."

"Why do you think that?"

"Because I just left with him. I knew I shouldn't, but I just did it."

"But you were a child. You were just six years old."

"Yeah."

"That is a lot of pressure you are putting on your six-year-old self." Linda nodded with tears in her eyes. "You have a son now, right? How old is he?"

"Yes, I do. He is six years old, almost seven."

"So he is the same age as you were back then." Linda nodded again. "Let me ask you this then: Would you blame him if he had been in your shoes? Would you think it would be his fault?" Linda cried and shook her head. "Why not?"

"Be- because he- he's just a kid. He is just a child." She was full on sobbing now.

"So the reasoning you are using to protect your child is not valid when it comes to yourself. Why do you think that is?"

"I don't know. I guess I tend to put a lot of pressure on myself."

"Maybe you feel like you don't quite deserve an out. Maybe you don't quite feel worthy enough."

"Yeah, I think you are right. I should probably work on that." She masked off her pain with a laugh and knew her therapist would see right through it.

"Well, we are reaching the end of our session. It was a lot today; how are you feeling?"

"Overwhelmed, but I also feel lighter in some way. For so long, I haven't been able to remember what happened back then. I have had nightmares about it and created scenarios in my head. Though the truth is scary, it is nice to know it. It feels good to be aware of it. I think, once this has settled in, a lot of things will make sense to me. The way I react to things, my fear of baths. They make sense now."

CHAPTER 20

Being without Tucker for the weekend was tough, and on top of the therapy session, Linda found herself in the need for some company. She thought about who to call, but the truth was that she didn't have any close friends to call. Her job had made it impossible to keep any friendships alive. Aside from Arnold, his wife Annelise, and Linda's brother and sister, she didn't really have anyone. She had grown close with Iversen and thought about calling him, but she feared it would give him the wrong idea. She wasn't ready to go through that again. She looked at her phone and hovered over Andrea's name for a while before thinking the better of it. Calling her would just result in a lot of questions. Besides, it was Saturday; Andrea was probably spending her day with her girlfriend, like she should be. And Linda was not strong enough for the rejection.

Instead of calling anyone, she went to the kitchen and opened a bottle of wine.

One more night, just one more night, and her boy would be back in her arms. She could do one more night. She emptied the glass and turned on some music. Got up from the couch and started dancing around. She was home alone, blinds were closed, and she felt safe. A smile spread across her lips, and she decided to do something she hadn't done in many years: dance around in her underwear.

She remembered the days when her siblings had been home from college and they danced around the house. Music blasted through the speakers, and they just had fun. They were always good at including her, and she was very grateful for that. Trish had always been good at checking in. Even if she had been out to a party with her friends, she would always text Linda goodnight and ask her about her day. She had been such a great sister and probably Linda's biggest support system, even when they were arguing. *God, I miss you so much.*

"What is happening here?" Linda jumped and covered herself with a pillow.

"Andrea," she exclaimed. "What are you doing here?"

"I'm sorry. I didn't mean to startle you. I just came to check up on you and to apologise."

"You came to check up on me?"

"Yes, Arnold called. I know he shouldn't be, but he is worried about you, and so am I."

"Yeah, yeah, me too."

"I heard the music and tried knocking, but I figured you couldn't hear me, so I tried the door and … did you know your door is unlocked? I guess you do now, since I am standing here. Anyway, I just …"

"Andrea," Linda said softly, and Andrea looked at her. "You are rambling."

"Right, sorry." Andrea blushed slightly. "Sorry, I should just go. Sorry." She turned to leave, but Linda tossed a pillow after her.

"Stay, please," she begged and went to grab another glass for her guest. "Unless of course you have to get back? I mean, it is Saturday night; you probably have to get back. You were always very adamant that weekends were reserved for family. You probably should go spend it with your girlfriend."

She hadn't intended to sound jealous, but now that the words were out of her mouth, she could hear it herself. She made a mental note to kick herself later and just hoped Andrea didn't notice.

"Who is rambling now?" Andrea chuckled and accepted the wine. "Actually, I would love to stay." STOP1

"Thank you, I'd really appreciate that. It has been tough with Tucker gone. I have been used to spending close to every second of every day with him, and now he is off with people I don't even know. I probably sound like a crazy person, but it is scary."

Andrea shook her head slightly.

"No, you don't sound crazy; you sound like his mother. A normal, concerned mother." Linda smiled at that.

"Thank you, I didn't know I needed to hear that. I mean, Arnold and Annelise have called me his mother, but I guess I just needed to hear it from someone else. So thank you."

Linda put her clothes back on, and they took a seat on the couch. Jealousy took ahold of her again, and she couldn't help but ask, "So what does your girlfriend think of you spending a Saturday night with your ex-wife?"

She didn't really want to hear the answer, but her mind wouldn't stop digging. Maybe this was her new way of self-sabotage: getting to know every detail of her ex-wife's new relationship. *God, I am such a self-sabotaging narcissist.*

"Well, actually, that is one of the reasons I came here today. I feel like I should explain, especially after the other night."

"You don't have to," Linda said and poured some more wine.

"No, I want to," Andrea insisted. "I first want to apologise for my behaviour that night. I don't remember much, but when I woke up, I had a vague memory of you bringing me home. I honestly thought it was a dream, but then Maddy confirmed it. She was a bit upset with me, said I had been all over you. You, on the other hand, had been a real gentlewoman and kept the boundaries clear." She smiled and chuckled a little. "It doesn't surprise me at all. You have always been the better person." Linda was about to comment, but Andrea held up her hand and continued, "Please, I need to get this all out." She took a sip of the wine and set it aside. "Firstly, I am really sorry for overstepping any boundaries that night. I know I was drunk, but that is no excuse. You were very kind to me, and I imagine I didn't make it very easy for you, and for that, I am very sorry." She took a shaky breath and looked down at her hands, trying to find the courage to continue. "Secondly, I want to apologise for Maddy. I didn't know she would be in the apartment. She had no reason to be. She and I are not— she is not my girlfriend; she and I are not an item."

"It is okay; you are free to date whoever you want."

"Yes, but I don't want you to think I am seeing anyone. We have been terrible at communicating, and I want us to be better at that. I remember what I said to you outside my apartment door—"

"Andrea," Linda began, not sure she was ready to have this conversation, but Andrea continued, determined to get it all out there.

"I love you," she said simply, and Linda felt her heart jump out of her chest. "I have never stopped loving you. Love was never an issue with us. I didn't ask for a divorce because I fell out of love with you. I just need you to know that."

Linda nodded, not quite sure what to say.

"Again, I am sorry if I have overstepped any boundaries. I just didn't want you to think I had moved on, because I haven't. I am not sure I ever will. I know it has been almost four years now, and we have both changed as individuals, and it is probably not fair of me to say this, but I still love you. You are it for me. And I am not asking you to get back together with me, I am certainly not expecting you to. I just wanted to tell you, in case, in case you feel the same way. I mean, you will never get what you want if you don't dare to risk it all, right?"

She tried to read Linda's face, but the more she tried, the more nervous she got. Her mind and body screamed for her to get out of there, to stop making a fool out of herself, but her heart begged her to stay, to wait just one more moment. Just one. Her heart won, and she stayed. Just one more moment. She was about to bolt, when Linda reached for her hand.

"Thank you for telling me," Linda started. "I am not sure I am ready to unpack all of that just yet. A lot has happened, and I have started therapy again. But I really do appreciate you being honest with me, and I want to give you the same level of honesty back. I just—" She felt a lump in her throat and had to take a moment. "I have really missed you." She broke out into a sob, and Andrea scooted closer to wipe away her tear. "I have missed my friend. I have missed my partner, my companion, my wife. Losing Gran was rough, but losing Trish … I still don't know how to put that into words. I have really missed someone to process it all with, and not just someone; I have missed you."

"I have missed you too," Andrea whispered, and Linda smiled.

"I am not in a great place right now. I am working on getting better, for myself and for Tucker. That boy has saved my life in more ways than one, and I have missed having someone to share that with. And I am also not saying that we should get back together. I think there is still a long way for us to go before we get there. But I would really love it if we could start talking more. Maybe get to know each other again. Is that something you would want?" Linda asked.

She wanted much more than that, especially seeing Andrea there in front of her, but she needed to work on herself more before she could go there. She deserved to love herself fully before she threw that love at someone else.

"I would like that." Andrea squeezed her hand. "I would like that very much."

CHAPTER 21

Watching Tucker get dropped off at home after his school trip filled Linda with a sense of hope. He had gone away on a trip without her and come back unharmed. It made her relax for a moment, thinking they were safe, thinking they had gotten away and now they could finally start their lives. It was a nice feeling, though she didn't allow it to linger for long. Anxiety and past experiences had taught her that bad things happened when you let your guards down. The moment you relaxed and felt comfortable was the moment the universe decided to test you. She knew it, yet she couldn't help but seek out that feeling again, occasionally.

"What do you wish for your birthday?" Linda asked Tucker, who put on his thinking face.

It was something he had picked up from school. He said his maths teacher had the same look whenever Tucker asked him questions. Tucker loved maths; it was by far his favourite subject. He was good at it too. Linda had been surprised during their home-schooling lessons. Reading and writing was a different story. He was way behind the other kids, and the school talked about having him tested for dyslexia. Linda blamed herself. Math had been easy for her to teach him, and he had been able to sit in peace with his task book. Reading demanded her attention, and with Nate around, they had always been interrupted. Maybe if she had been given Tucker more attention during that time, he would be better at reading and writing now.

She was pulled from her thoughts when Tucker spoke.

"An ankylosaurus," Tucker said after much consideration.

"A what now?" Linda asked, dumbfounded. *How does he even know that word?*

"Ankylosaurus," Tucker repeated and wrote it down. Linda's eyes widened. *Wait, he can spell that? Since when can he spell that?* "See?" He spoke and pointed to the word. "An-kyl-o-saurus. Ankylosaurus."

"Is that a dinosaur?" Linda asked and felt a bit stupid. Apparently that was a stupid question because Tucker threw his head back and started laughing like it was common knowledge. Linda smiled. God, she loved that boy.

"Yes," Tucker giggled and pushed the paper away so he could continue helping with the birthday cake.

"Hmm, I don't know if we can fit a dinosaur in here. Is it one of the small ones?" Linda asked. Tucker started laughing again and shook his head.

"No, Mommy, they don't exist anymore. They are instinquished." He concentrated on stirring the butter to get it melted.

"I think you mean 'extinct,'" Linda corrected him with a smile and prepared a bowl for the dry ingredients. "Do you want to use the scale?"

Tucker quickly left the butter and jumped on the counter to pour the flour. He had his thinking face on again. Linda watched as his tongue slid out the side of his mouth, really focusing on not spilling the flour.

"So if you know that dinosaurs are extinct, then how can you get one for your birthday?" she asked and helped him collect the ingredients in the bowl for him to stir.

"Not a real one, Mommy. But Timothy in school has a T-Rex on his wall."

"And you would like an …" She skimmed over at the paper to remember the name again. "Ankylosaurus on your bedroom wall?"

Tucker nodded and added the egg she handed him, while she poured some milk in.

"Okay, I think that would be a great idea. But I don't know what this dinosaur looks like, so you will have to explain it to me. Is it one of those with sharp teeth, because they are scary."

"They are called carnivorous," Tucker explained.

Where is this knowledge coming from? Linda thought to herself and made a mental note to brush up on her dino-knowledge.

"How do you know that?" she asked.

"We talked about it in school, and we went to a museum. They had a real dinosaur! Then we had to draw our favourite and show it to the class. The ankylosaurus is my favourite. Timothy's favourite is the tyrannosaurus rex. It is a carnivore dinosaur, so it eats meat. That is also Brett's favourite. Anna's favourite is the triceratops. It is an herbivore dinosaur, like my favourite, so it is vegetarian like us."

He smiled, and Linda had to give him a kiss on the cheek. He was definitely getting a dinosaur on his wall, no question.

Tucker watched the cake the whole time it was in the oven. He pulled over his beanbag and placed it in front of the oven and watched it like a movie. "It is growing. Mommy, it's growing. Look," he shouted and pointed at the oven. Linda smiled to herself and continued folding the laundry. "It is getting colour too," he continued, and at that, Linda decided, *To hell with the chores,* and took a seat next to him on the floor. Tucker was growing up so fast, and she figured they would only have a limited number of moments like these.

They sat in silence and watched the cake rise. She was quite surprised at how evenly it rose and felt a sense of pride watching the magic at work.

"Mommy, was my dad a bad man?" Tucker suddenly asked.

Linda was a little startled by his question. They hadn't really talked about Nate. Linda had meant to bring it up, but she hadn't quite known how to. Part of her had hoped she wouldn't have to, but of course she had to. Nate was Tucker's father, and he always would be, regardless of what he did or what kind of man he was.

"Why do you ask that?"

"Benjamin at school said so. His dad is a police officer and said that my dad had done some bad thing, so he wasn't allowed to play with me."

Linda felt her stomach knot and wanted to tread carefully here.

"Benjamin's dad shouldn't have said that," she started. *I am definitely finding out what Benjamin's last name is,* Linda thought, wanting to have a stern conversation with this police officer. "It is wrong to judge someone based on someone else's actions. Did Benjamin say what kind of bad things your dad was doing?"

Tucker nodded slowly.

"He said my dad hurt women."

"I see, and do you believe that?"

"He hurt you," he stated simply and turned his head back towards the oven.

"Yes," Linda whispered. "But he is not hurting me or anyone else anymore, okay?"

Tucker nodded and rested his head against her shoulder.

"It is okay to miss him, you know? It is okay if you want to talk about him. He was your dad, and he loved you very much."

Tucker was quiet for a bit, then spoke.

"Do you miss him?" he asked.

"Sometimes," Linda answered honestly.

Nate wasn't all bad; granted his few good traits rarely saw the light of day, but there had been a few good moments. But more importantly, she missed Tucker having a father. Tucker had loved his dad, and no child should go through losing their parent that early on.

"I miss him too," Tucker said quietly, and Linda wrapped her arm around him.

"We can talk about him, if you want."

"No, I just miss him is all."

"And that is completely okay. But you can always come to me and talk about him if you want to. I will always be here to listen."

Tucker looked at her and nodded, then turned his eyes back on the cake.

"Do you think it is done now?" he asked, pointing at the oven. Just as he spoke, the timer went off, and Tucker jumped to his feet. "Mmm. It smells so good." He smiled and leaned over the steaming cake.

"Tucker, are the other kids at school talking about your dad?" Linda asked, worried that Nate's actions would continue to affect him.

"No, Anna threatened them. She and Brett said they would kick their asses if they talked about my dad again." Tucker smiled.

Linda chuckled at that; she could easily imagine little Anna making tight fists and walking up to the bigger kids and being threatening, despite her tiny size. She was a feisty one, and with Brett backing her up, Linda felt her son was in safe hands.

She again allowed herself to relax and feel safe, this time ignoring the anxiety and nagging feeling that something bad would happen if she kept this up. She was tired of being scared, tired of running. Life was good to them now, and it was easy to feel safe. They deserved to feel safe, deserved to be happy.

She fell asleep that night with a smile on her face and peace in her heart, slept soundly for the first time in many years. No nightmares or terrors; she probably didn't even dream. She just slept and felt content. She even turned in her sleep and faced away from the door. She had never turned in her sleep before, not since she was a child. Her body had always been frozen in the same position every night and her mind always alert, even in her dreams. She had never given her body and mind away like this. Never allowed herself to give in and let her unconscious state overtake her fully. She had always been a light sleeper and woke at the slightest sound or even puff of wind. But not tonight. Tonight, she felt safe. She felt comfortable and relaxed, happy.

She was happy.

CHAPTER 22

The wind was roaring loudly and threatening from above. The rain fell heavily, and every drop echoed through the night as it hit the ground. An old oak tree creaked like a warning while a few birds took off. Iversen felt his jacket soaked through from the rain, and droplets were dripping from his nose. He was standing in the driveway to the house. The forest trees and darkness made the place secluded and safe. No one was around for miles; no one would catch him. The house was dark and quiet; only the sound of wind from outside could be heard.

He made his way around the back of the house. He had noticed the old porch door last time he was there. He figured that would be the easiest way in. Wet footsteps followed him through the house, and his sneakers creaked quietly on the hardwood floors.

He sneaked down the hallway and stopped at the first door on his right. *Tucker*, it read with orange letters on the door. Iversen slowly turned the knob and looked inside. Tucker was sleeping in his bed, sprawled out like a starfish on his stomach. He had pushed the covers off during the night, and they had fallen to the floor, his bare legs exposed to the cool temperature of the room.

Iversen walked over to the bed and looked down at the boy. The moon allowed enough light to make out the various scars and bruises on the boy's body. Iversen had heard about Linda's time undercover and figured this boy had been through more than most. In many ways, he recognised himself in this boy, and he found himself apologising to the kid for what he was about to do. He bent over and gently touched the skin of Tucker's leg. The skin was cold under his touch, and he looked at the fallen covers on the floor. He picked them up and covered the boy, before he walked back out and gently closed the door behind him.

He hoped Tucker was a heavy sleeper; he wouldn't want to have to hurt the little boy.

The room across from Tucker's was the bedroom. Excitement and goosebumps rushed through Iversen's body as he approached the door, knowing Linda would be asleep inside. He leaned his head against it and smiled, felt aroused by the thought of being so close to her. His angel.

He prepared himself and opened the door. Expected Linda to jump out of bed at the sound, and Iversen would finally reveal to her that he was the Angel Maker and that he had been all along. He expected a fight, one he would win, and he would finally be reunited with his angel.

He walked in and stood tall, wanting to look as intimidating as possible. He smiled in anticipation and coughed slightly, in case she hadn't heard the door. No movement was seen from the bed, no startled sounds. Just the slow rise of her shoulder as she was breathing and the gentle sound of her breath. *She still sleeping. How can she still be sleeping?* Initially, he was annoyed, but the realisation made him bolder, and he walked closer to her bed. She was sleeping on her side, the covers loosely falling over her body, her hands tucked under her pillow, and her hair spilling everywhere. Her breath was steady and calm. She didn't even know he was there. The knowledge pulled further at Iversen's arousal as he thought of a million different things he could do.

He sat down on the bed next to her and pulled lightly on the covers. His eyes widened as her deep scars on her back were revealed. "My angel," he whispered. "It is really you." His hands were shaking, and he didn't dare breathe as his fingers ghosted over the scars. "Wings," he said with a smile and tucked the covers down further, exposing her entire back.

He remembered giving her wings, remembered every cut. She had been drugged the whole time, hadn't as much as moved under his touch. Iversen was sure she had enjoyed it. He was sure she had felt the same arousal he had. She had to, right?

He traced the scarring with his flashlight and smiled with his eyes wide. The symmetry was poignant. He had really taken his time, made sure the wings were even on both sides, even down to the depth of each cut. It was beautiful, a true masterpiece, his very best work, and soon everyone would know. They would all see him for the artist that he was, and he would finally get the recognition he deserved. It had pained him when that old bastard had been arrested and found guilty of all the crimes he had committed. All of his hard work had just been given to that fool, who had no imagination or purpose in this life. Iversen had almost given himself up, almost. Then he recognised the possibilities here. Maybe that old fool finally had a purpose. The old man would take the blame for now, and in the meantime, Iversen had been able to perfect his work.

He had thought about quitting, but it had been too hard. The rush of the kill had been too thrilling, too delicious. It was like putting candy in front of a child. The temptation to take a piece was too great, and once you had had the taste of one, you wanted another. Then another, and before you knew it, you were on a binge. Addicted to the sweetness, and not even the strongest could say no.

He took out a Polaroid camera from his pocket and snapped a photo of her. Then he took another, just for safekeeping, and put it in his pocket.

It would be so easy to end it now. She was right there, served to him on a plate like a delicious dessert; he just had to take a bite. The temptation was strong. He knew this would be the sweetest taste of all time, but maybe this was not meant to be yet. Maybe he was meant to wait a little longer. Just a little.

He closed his eyes and felt release. Let himself enjoy this moment a little while longer before he disappeared out of the room. His wet footsteps still visible on the floor and the porch door still broken from his entry. It excited him, knowing that when they woke up, they would know someone had been there. They would know that the real killer was still out here. Just as they were relaxing, he would turn their worlds upside down again. Knowing that made him smile wide; he couldn't wait to comfort Linda tomorrow, hold her and tell her that everything would be okay, help ease the dark times, knowing that he was the darkness all along.

Linda woke with a smile that morning. She hadn't slept that well in a long time. Tucker was still asleep when she peeked in on him; she would let him snooze a little while longer before he had to get up and get ready for school.

She went into the kitchen, put on a pot of coffee, and made her way back to the bedroom to get dressed. Her subconscious noticed the open porch door, but she was still too groggy to give it any real attention. While brushing her teeth and walking to wake up Tucker, her eyes fell on the door next to Tucker's room. The name *Willa* was written on the door with purple letters, and underneath it was a dancing unicorn. She smiled slightly and called for Tucker, helped him get ready for the day.

"Mommy, why is there water on the floor?" Tucker asked and pointed to the halfway-dried footsteps in the kitchen.

Linda studied them closer and found the porch door open. The storm had been rough last night, so maybe the wind had knocked open the old door, and then a stray cat had taken shelter in their kitchen through the night. It looked like footsteps, but she pushed that thought away; she felt comfortable in the safe place now and didn't want to disrupt that, though she subconsciously knew something was wrong.

Tucker was picked up by his friend's dad and taken to school; she watched while he waved happily out the window. It still made Linda happy to see her son thrive in this new life.

The good feeling filled her that morning, and she dared to do something she hadn't done in a long time. She walked to Willa's room and opened the door, sat on Willa's bed for the first time since her death, and took a deep breath. She hadn't been able to open the bedroom door, let alone step into the space, for a long time.

She and Andrea had discussed selling the house after their divorce, but Linda hadn't been able to go through with it. It was a sacred space now, the last testament to Willa ever having existed.

For a long time after the accident, this house had been all Linda saw. This was where she had been since everything fell apart, moving around the halls like a zombie, ordering takeaway, and closing herself off from everyone.

She touched the bedsheets under her, closed her eyes, and let her hand caress the material. The bed was covered in a quilt. Every little square had a memory. Willa and Andrea had surprised Linda with it for her birthday. The material was cut from Willa's baby clothes, and now it was Linda's most treasured possession.

She stood from the bed and made her way to the dresser at the opposite side of the room. She opened a drawer and ran her hands along the garments that would go unworn. She spotted Willa's favourite shirt, a simple white blouse with small pearls around the neckline. She remembered going to the mall with her wife and child. Andrea had spotted the shirt from across the store and had insisted on getting it. Willa, of course, being just like her mamma, had refused to take it off once she had tried it on. The cashier had to scan the label with Willa wearing the shirt and proudly showing off her new blouse.

A tear fell from the corner of her eye. Willa would never get to wear it again. Eventually, Linda would box it up and store it somewhere, maybe give it to goodwill. Take Willa's paintings down, pack up her toys and knick-knacks. She would shove them in her car and take them with her when she moved. Eventually, just not yet.

Until then, she would continue to let her anguish stir and burn inside her till it was finally time to move on. And probably even still.

She shook her head, found the memories to be too much. She was about to make her way out of there, when she noticed one of Willa's teddy bears on the floor.

"Mr. Teddy," Linda whispered. "What are you doing down there?" She picked him up and dusted him off. "Did you have a fight with Mrs. Teddy? Cause you are supposed to sit right here next to ..." She narrowed her eyes on the bed. "... her." She finished but couldn't see Mrs. Teddy anywhere.

All colour drained from her face. Mr. Teddy fell to the floor once more, and Linda had to grab the wall for support. Mrs. Teddy was missing, and in her place was a stack of Polaroid photos. The front one was a photo of herself sleeping with her back bare, exposing the scars she had spent her whole life hiding. There was something written on the bottom, but she couldn't see it properly from where she was standing.

She took an unsteady step and reached for the photo. Her hands shaking and her heart hammering as she read the words: "All angels have wings."

CHAPTER 23

It felt like the phone was ringing forever. One long slow call tone after the other. "Pick up … pick up," she whispered and bared her teeth, her jaw tightened and her shaky hand gripped tighter around the phone. "Please, pick up. Please, please, please." Her foot started tapping on the floor, and she closed her eyes to let her prayer sink in, but it went unanswered. She tried again. Called the same number, and this time started walking around outside. Again, no answer.

She had almost lost hope when her phone suddenly rang. Relief washed over her at the sight of Arnold's name on the caller ID. "Arnold," she exclaimed as she put the phone to her ear. "Arnold, I need you to help me, please." She struggled to get the words out. "He is back. Arnold, he is back. The Angel Maker, he is still out there." She grew frantic and started hyperventilating.

Arnold had been on his way to the lake for a fishing trip. Annelise had kicked him out of the house and told him go find a hobby. She had even asked him if the station couldn't use his experience as a consultant on some cases. He had laughed at that. For years, she had begged him to come home and stop working such long hours, and now that he was home, she was begging him to return to work.

He had never imagined that he would in fact return to work, but if what Linda was saying was true, then his work was not over; his job was not done.

Linda had started hyperventilating on the phone and he knew there was no talking her down till he was there with her. It had been a while since she had experienced a panic attack, but whatever had scared her, seemed to have scared her good.

He reached her home in ten minutes and called out for her, as he entered the house.

"Linda? Linda where are you? It is me, Arnold." He heard silent cries from the kitchen and made his way through., embraced the young woman, and tried to calm her down. She was shaking uncontrollably and clung to him like her life depended on it. Her reaction scared him, made him think this was real, that the Angel Maker really was out there still and they had apprehended the wrong guy.

"He is back," she whispered after a while, her body still shaking and her voice still coarse from crying.

"He can't be. We caught him, remember?" Arnold tried but didn't quite believe it himself.

"He is back," she just said again. She got up, walked to the hallway, and stopped outside Willa's room.

Arnold silently followed.

"He was here last night. While we were sleeping. He broke in through the porch door and went into our rooms. He was in Willa's room, my room." She turned to Arnold. "Tucker's! He was in Tucker's room and took photos of him in his sleep." She pointed to the Polaroids on Willa's bed.

Arnold walked into the room and looked down on the bed. A few photos were sprayed on the bedding while the rest were still neatly stacked. One photo was of Tucker in his bed, and another was of Linda in hers. The pictures in themselves were chilling enough. But what made Arnold petrified was the little sentence written at the bottom of the photo of Linda in her bed with her back uncovered.

"All angels have wings," Arnold read, and Linda took a step back.

She was right, he was back. Or as it turned out, he had never left in the first place. They had the wrong guy. Why that was, they had to investigate, but for now, the most important thing was to give Linda and Tucker protection.

"Have you touched anything?" Arnold asked, and Linda nodded. "Okay, let's go back to the kitchen and make a list of everything you have touched."

Linda nodded and was the first one to walk back to the kitchen.

"Could you make us some coffee, then I will just give a call to the team?" Arnold asked, knowing that keeping her busy would distract her from the situation and keep her thoughts busy for a while. "Is there anyone else you want me to call? Do you want Annelise to come over?"

"I don't want to be a burden to anyone."

"Please," Arnold said, before she had a change to finish. "You are family, and you could never be a burden. I will call Annelise." He smiled softly at her. "I haven't had anything to eat yet; could I trouble you for some breakfast? Looks like we have a long day ahead of us."

"Yes, of course." Linda opened the fridge and found some eggs and toast. Figured the stove and kitchen equipment were alright to touch, as both her and Tucker had already done so earlier that morning.

Arnold left her to it and walked out of ear-range before he pulled out his phone.

"Iversen?" he said and felt a lump in his throat. "I need you to gather the team for me and bring them to Linda's place."

"Linda's? Why? Did something happen? Is she okay?" His concerned voice sounded on the other end.

"Don't worry. She is not hurt; not yet."

"What do you mean, 'not yet,' Buch? What is happening?"

Iversen sounded like a concerned boyfriend, and it made Arnold smile despite everything. He had never seen Iversen this protective over anyone, and though he did not think them to be a match, it was still refreshing to see the young man care for someone other than himself.

"We got the wrong guy. The Angel Maker, it is not Mr. Cooper. I am not sure how the young man is involved in all of this, but he is not the real Angel Maker."

"How is that possible? Everything we have points to him."

Arnold took a deep breath. He wasn't sure how it happened. He wasn't sure of anything anymore.

"It pains me to admit this, but I think most of our evidence would fit with just about anyone. The most compelling pieces we have on him is the witness statement against him and his own confession, but it could all have been a lie, a ploy to cover for the truth, allowing the real killer to roam free and keep searching for Linda."

He cursed himself and knew now that this was the truth. Hearing it spoken out loud and with everything that had just happened, there had to be more to it than that. Catching Cooper had been too easy. It hadn't felt right, and now he knew why. It wasn't right. It was all a lie to cover the truth, to lead them to this moment.

The Angel Maker had played them all along. He had a plan, and they had fallen into it, followed it to a tee.

His anger was split between frustration and fascination. He had been played back then, and now he had been played again. Maybe he was right to retire; maybe he was off his game, getting too old for this. He considered stepping back, letting Iversen do it; maybe it would be for the best.

He called Annelise next.

"Don't tell me you forgot something?" Annelise's voice sounded on the phone. *She is still annoyed*, Arnold thought to himself with a chuckle but pushed the thought aside; they had other more important matters to discuss right now.

"I need you to come to Linda's." His tone was clear, and he could sense the seriousness falling over his wife as he spoke. "She needs every little bit of family we can muster right now."

"What has happened?" Annelise asked with genuine concern in her voice. "Is she okay?"

"She is okay, but she and Tucker will need to stay with us for a couple of days. It is safer that way. I will explain everything when you get here. This one is easier face-to-face." Annelise seemed to agree and was already headed out the door when Arnold continued, "Call Andrea too, will you?"

"Say no more; I got it covered," Annelise assured him and shared a silent moment with her husband before she hung up and called Andrea.

Iversen and the team were there within minutes, and they went through the house from top to bottom. Arnold handed them the list of everything they had touched and where they had been sitting or standing, so they knew where the crime scene potentially had been contaminated. Arnold and Linda were escorted out of the house and waited by the car till Annelise arrived. She was to take Linda with her back to their house, and once the evidence was secured, Arnold would give Linda a call to pack her and Tucker a bag so they could stay with Arnold and Annelise for the week.

Annelise drove them back home and made sure to keep Linda busy, made sure to distract her, keep her mind occupied with small mundane tasks. Linda accepted it, went into autopilot. Her survival instincts kicked in, and protective walls were quickly built around her. She had allowed herself to relax, and now bad things were happening again. This wouldn't happen again; it couldn't.

She had given in to the temptation of feeling safe, and she had ignored the nagging feeling telling her to stay alert. She had disregarded the anxiety and all the warning signs. She had even brushed off the distressing feeling this morning when she had found the porch door opened. There had been footsteps in her kitchen, and she had been so content in her little happy bubble that she had brushed it off as a stray cat seeking shelter from the storm.

"It is my fault," she whispered. "It is all my fault."

Annelise heard her and assured her otherwise, but she knew that Linda wasn't listening. Linda blamed herself, and she would continue to do so until it was all over. Annelise just hoped it would be sooner rather than later and that there would be no more scary surprises. For once, she was hoping Arnold would go back to work and finish what he had started. This guy needed catching, and none of them would be getting any sleep till he was captured or killed.

A knock on the door startled them both, till Annelise remember that she had phoned Andrea for assistance.

"Where is she?" Andrea asked as soon as Annelise opened the door.

"She is in the kitchen. She is peeling potatoes for tonight. I was trying to keep her busy," Annelise explained and watched as the woman rushed through the house in her search for the kitchen.

"Linda," Andrea exclaimed and watched as her ex-wife stopped in her tracks at the sound of her voice.

As she looked up and their eyes met, Linda's whole body relaxed and gave in to the panicking feeling. Andrea was quick and engrossed her in a tight hug before a mentally broken Linda collapsed in her arms.

"I am here, my love. I am here," Andrea whispered and just held her tighter. "You are safe now; I got you."

A quiet "Thank you" made its way over Linda's lips in between the sobs.

"Always, my love. Always."

CHAPTER 24

It had been a rough night for all of them. Tucker had a hard time understanding why he could not sleep in his own bed and why they couldn't go home, and Linda had not been in a state to explain it all to him, as she barely understood it herself. Annelise and Arnold had been kind and understanding as always and had made up one of the spare bedrooms for them to stay as long as they needed to. Their home was always open to Linda and Tucker, and even Andrea had been welcomed to stay the night.

Despite having a big house with plenty of rooms and beds, they had all camped out in the living room. Tucker snuggled up against Linda on the couch, with Andrea not long out of reach, Arnold in his recliner and Annelise on the other couch. They would all wake with sore backs in the morning, but it had felt comforting to be close this first night. They had needed each other, and all needed to feel safe despite what was going on.

Linda had struggled to fall asleep. She kept staring at the ceiling and stealing glances at the people around her, as sleep overtook them. Not daring to leave anyone out of sight. Even as she closed her eyes, her body was still awake, still alert. She needed to stay awake, in case he came back. This time, she would be prepared. This time, he would not get to lay a hand on either of them.

She felt her arms instinctively wrap around Tucker and hold him tight. Andrea's body seemed to have felt the movement and wrapped herself around Linda like a blanket. It made Linda smile for a moment, and she relaxed a bit. Just enough to allow sleep to take over. Her body was still tense, still alert, but she knew they were safe. She had Tucker in her arms, she herself was wrapped in Andrea's, with Arnold and Annelise just a few feet away. Outside were officers protecting them, and all the windows and doors were locked. Though even in her sleep she couldn't help but feel like this security wasn't enough to keep them safe. They were safe for now, but for how long? The Angel Maker was still out there, and if he had proven anything, it was that he was not one to give up. If anything, when met with a challenge, it just seemed to motivate him further. How was she going to stop that? How was she supposed to win against that?

Another nagging thought in her sleep told her he would be able to get to her, even in the safest of places. He was like a wolf in sheep clothing. He had gotten into her house so easily; who was to say that he hadn't done it before, and that he wouldn't do it again?

To ease her concerns, they had put her house under twenty-four-hour surveillance in case the Angel Maker decided to make a return.

Iversen was leading the investigation, giving him another excellent opportunity to control the chess pieces, knowing every move and countermove. He knew he had to get Linda alone, and that Arnold would not leave her out of his sight until they had made significant progress in the investigation. Alternatively, if he could guarantee her safety, she would move back home, and he would have direct access to her again.

Regret washed over him as he thought back on last night. He had her right where he wanted her and yet he failed to take the final step. He had wanted to so badly, but more so, he had wanted to continue the dance of theirs, continue the pursuit. As long as no one knew he was the real Angel Maker, then he held all the power. Linda might be safe now, but holding all that power made him feel good, godlike, as if God himself was reaching out to him, telling him to continue his work, to keep making angels, giving them wings, and sending them on their way to the Promised Land, where God would take them in as his own.

He would continue his quest. Continue until he himself joined God and all his angels, and they would treat him with the respect he deserved, look at him as their maker and saviour.

He could take Linda. He had the power, but he wanted her to join him of her own free will. She was his angel, and she belonged to him. He just needed to get her to see that. He needed to break her just a little more. Send her over the edge and then pick up the pieces, make her dependent on him, and he knew just the way.

He was talking with Arnold in the kitchen while the others played Ludo with Tucker in the living room. They were discussing the case as new sensitive information had come to light.

A woman and her child had been found murdered in their home. Everything about it was so brutal and cold that it could only have been one person: the Angel Maker. Arnold read the note that had been left in the hand of the murdered woman and felt chills run down his spine. This woman and her child had done nothing wrong; they had done nothing to provoke him. The woman simply looked like Linda, and as a way to assert dominance and inflict pain and fear, she had been killed.

"Don't let Linda see this," he whispered to Iversen and tucked the letter between two documents. "She doesn't need this. Not right now."

Iversen nodded and gathered up the files when there was a knock on the door. Outside was a woman with a stern look, along with some police officers.

"What can I do for you?" he asked, purposefully keeping his voice down to avoid attracting attention from Linda and the others inside.

However, Linda was already listening in. She had already heard the two of them whispering in the kitchen and had gone to take a look at the files she had been forbidden to see.

Iversen had abandoned the files to assist Arnold with the strangers, and Linda was left alone with pictures of a woman and her child. Both had been raped repeatedly and drowned, mutilated after their deaths. The sight made her sick, and she had to run to the sink. The sound brought Arnold back into the kitchen, where he quickly came to the aid of his friend and sent Iversen a look saying, "Why the hell did you leave these files out? Pack it up, now!" Iversen didn't need to hear the actual words to understood that look, and he quickly collected everything again, but not before accidentally spilling the letter on the floor and purposefully not seeing it till Linda had already picked it up.

"What is this? Why is it addressed to me?"

Arnold snapped his head up at the question and saw Linda holding the very thing she was not supposed to see. She was in a fragile state, and this could take her over the edge. Arnold again snapped his eyes to Iversen, and if looks could kill, Iversen could consider himself sucker-punched by the look Arnold was giving him. Iversen, of course, knew exactly what he was doing, and while he was smiling on the inside, his demeanour stayed that of the handsome and trustworthy Iversen.

"Linda Marie Hemmer," it read on the envelope. Linda unfolded the letter with shaky hands, and despite Arnold's objections, she started reading.

> My angel, my sweet, sweet angel.
> I found you. I finally found you.
> I found you after all this time.
> All the women I have killed,
> All the lives that have been spilled,
> Just in the search for you!
> My angel, my sweet angel.
> I found you. I know you.
> I found your home and your heart.
> All the people in your life.
> All the people you love.
> In danger, just because of you!
> My angel, my sweet angel.
> I found you. I will not stop.
> All the plans I have for us.
> All the damage I can still do.
> All of it, all I will do for you!

"What is all this?" a strange voice asked, and everyone turned their heads towards the door. The woman from before had entered the kitchen and stood there with two officers.

"I told you, now is not the time," Arnold spit out and positioned himself between Linda and the strangers.

"And I told you, Mr. Buch, that this cannot wait." She said his name with spite, like there was some history there still lingering.

"What is all this shouting?" Annelise asked as she entered the kitchen. Tucker and Andrea followed, both gravitating towards Linda at the sight of the strangers.

"Miss Danton?" Annelise asked and stood tall. "To what do we owe this pleasure?"

Her voice was polite, but it was clear that she did not like this woman, and Linda wondered what the story was there. Had Arnold and Miss Danton maybe dated in a past life?

"Mrs. Buch, a pleasure as always," the woman sneered and turned her attention towards Linda. "I am not here for you. I am here on official business, as it has come to our attention that Miss Hemmer has failed to fulfil her duties as Tucker's guardian."

"What?" They all snapped in unison, and Tucker hid behind Linda, sensing that this was not good.

"You are not taking him." The words were out of Linda's mouth before she could stop herself.

"Taking me? Where am I going?" Tucker asked, and Linda cursed herself. She looked at the boy with a smile and kissed his cheek.

"Nowhere, you are exactly where you are supposed to be." She said it with love and warmth, and looked at Andrea, who understood and dragged Tucker back to their Ludo game.

"I am afraid that was a lie you just told him," Danton objected once the child was out of earshot.

"You are not taking him," Linda said again. This time, her voice was firm and her fists clenched alongside her body. Arnold kept his position between the two, while Annelise put a calming hand on Linda's shoulder.

"I was very clear, if you at any point failed to keep young Tucker safe, then I would have no choice but to place him elsewhere. It is vital for his metal recovery that he is in a safe environment."

"I have kept him safe," Linda yelled and cursed herself again for having raised her voice.

"It disturbs me that this is what you call safe."

Arnold intervened and made some comments, but Danton said, "I am sorry, Mr. Buch, but I fail to see how that is relevant."

"Relevant? Of course, it is relevant. Linda has done nothing to deserve this; she is a victim in all this."

He was getting aggravated, and Annelise had to give him a warning touch. They couldn't deal with him getting a heart attack again on top of everything else.

"Victim or not, Mr. Buch, Miss Hemmer knew the rules, and she has failed to fulfil her duties. Not only has this serial killer been looking for Miss Hemmer for years, all the while killing innocent women, he has now also murdered a child. This before he gained access to Miss Hemmer's home, as she and Tucker were asleep. And now she has moved in with a retired police officer and his wife just to sleep safely at night. No. This is no situation for a child, let alone a child like young Tucker with his traumatic upbringing. He needs a stable environment, somewhere where he can feel safe and loved and not have to worry about himself or anyone else."

"He is loved," Arnold bit back and stepped closer, but Danton didn't seem fazed by his aggression, like she had seen it all before. To her, he was all bark and no bite, whereas she seemed to be all bite.

"I have no doubt that Miss Hemmer loves Tucker very much, which is also why I know she will do the right thing," Danton said and looked past Arnold, straight into Linda's eyes.

"The right thing? The right thing? How is taking that boy away from his mother the right thing?" Arnold yelled and caused a smile to appear on Danton's face, like she had been waiting for him to refer to Linda as Tucker's mother.

"Mr. Buch, let's not forget how we got in this mess in the first place, shall we? And you can spare me the speech of it being classified information because I know it all. Miss Hemmer, however good her intentions were, crossed a line while undercover, and her actions resulted in a child shooting and killing his own father to save her life. He may see her as his mother, but we all know that she is not. She is merely the only stable thing he has ever known, and he is only with her because she essentially kidnapped him." She held up her hand to stop Arnold and kept speaking. "Now, before you say anything, I am fully aware that her heroic actions saved young Tucker's life but that does not make her the best caretaker for this young boy."

Linda closed her eyes and released a breath. Danton was right, and as much as it pained her to admit, Tucker would be safer with someone else.

"Not to mention that Miss Hemmer failed to show in my office yesterday as part of the agreement when she took on the role of young Tucker's care."

"Yeah, because a serial killer was at her house," Iversen intervened with aggression.

"Which only goes to prove my point. This is no environment for a child. Now, if you will excuse me, I have a busy schedule, and Tucker is to meet with his new family in a few hours."

Arnold again started objecting and raging, but Linda stopped him. She stepped forward and motioned for Danton to follow her into the living room.

"Are they good people? The ones he is going to?" she asked quietly.

"They are wonderful. They have two other adopted children, and they have been looking for a third for a very long time. They have already set up his room."

Linda nodded and kept walking.

Tucker and Andrea were sitting on the floor, playing Ludo. They were both silent, and Linda figured their yelling in the kitchen had travelled through the house.

"Tucker," she said with a sad smile and sat down next to the boy. "I am sorry for all the yelling; we should have been able to have had that conversation without yelling."

Tucker crawled into her lap and wrapped his arms around her neck.

"Is it true what that lady said? Am I getting a new family?"

Linda's heart broke at his question, and she had to fight hard to keep it together. Andrea gave her hand a squeeze, and she lifted Tucker's cute little face from her chest.

"Yes, it is true," she whispered, mostly because she didn't have enough voice to speak properly. "Miss Danton here is going to take you to some people who are really excited to meet you. They have two other children, so you get to have siblings, and siblings are the best. You are going to live with them now, and they are going to love you so much."

Tucker looked at her with his eyebrows knitted together. He was quiet for a long time, looking like he was trying to solve a math problem in his head. Linda was about to say something when he finally seemed to have solved whatever he was trying to work out.

"So I get a new mommy and daddy and siblings?" he asked, and Linda felt a knot in her stomach, but smiled and nodded. "Then what about you? Will you not be my mommy anymore?"

"I will always love you, and I will always be with you right here." She covered his heart with her hand and kissed his cheek.

"But then who will take care of you?" he asked.

Linda closed her eyes and hugged him tightly. This was exactly what Danton meant. Tucker needed an environment where he could be a child, a place where he could feel safe and not worry about anything or anyone. He had never had that, not even with her.

CHAPTER 25

To say that the days after losing Tucker were rough was an understatement. Losing him left a hole in their family and especially a hole in Linda. Days passed, and with them, so did Tucker's birthday. Being around Arnold and Annelise, as lovely as they were, quickly became too much for Linda. All the looks and unspoken words of "How are you feeling? What do you need?" became a trigger for Linda, and she had to get out of there. She still worried about the Angel Maker and what would happen, but without Tucker, she just didn't seem to care anymore. Nothing seemed to matter. What happened to her was no longer important.

Tucker was safe, so she had done her job.

Arnold had insisted on following her home. He didn't want her to spend the day alone, especially not since it was Tucker's birthday, and he was worried what she would do. He also knew that she needed a break from him and his wife, so he didn't want to intrude. Reaching out to Andrea had opened a whole can of worms, and Linda had insisted that she could not be around Andrea right now. The two of them were still mending their bond, and everything that was happening right now felt too close to home. It was too familiar to what they had gone through together with Willa, and Linda was afraid it would cause her to snap and push Andrea away for good.

No, she needed this time for herself. She wanted to be by herself.

So Arnold did the next best thing, or so he thought. He asked his trusted partner for help. Shared his concerns with Iversen and asked him to keep an eye on Linda for the next couple of days. He would be parked out front of her home with a colleague to keep her safe, and he promised to do regular check-ins, making sure she didn't do anything reckless.

Linda was standing in her kitchen that afternoon, looking at the cake in the fridge. Tucker was supposed to have brought it to school a few days ago, as his birthday fell on a Sunday. She remembered the joy and laughter they had shared while making this cake. Looking at it now, it brought her nothing but sorrow. Tucker was gone, he was safe, but she would never see him again. His new parents had made that very clear when she had called to wish him a happy birthday.

"We are only allowing this because he keeps asking for you, and because it is his birthday, but you must stop calling. He lives with us now, and he cannot move on unless you move on."

That had been their response to her request, and after a short minute of talking with sweet Tucker, the line had been disconnected, and the phone had not been picked up since. Loneliness had tugged at her heart then, and she had broken down for the first time that day. Iversen had found her and carried her to bed. He must have tucked her in as well, cause when she woke, she was nice and warm, and the duvet hugged her in a comforting way.

She appreciated Iversen as a friend. He was good at being present without being in her face, and he just seemed to know what she needed, like he understood what she was going though. She had shared a little bit with him about her childhood and what the Angel Maker had done to her and how it had come to consume her life, and in contrast to Arnold, Iversen had not asked any intrusive questions. He had just listened and automatically been compassionate, like he had known what she had gone through. It had felt nice, and she had given him a big hug after that.

Iversen was a good guy; he had proven that time and time again, and as warm as it made Linda feel, it also made her feel guilty. Here he was, a decent guy who genuinely cared for her, and she would not give him the time of day. She knew how he felt for her, and yet she could not find it in herself to feel the same for him. She cared for him, as a friend, but it would never be more than that. It made her feel like a terrible person, even more so than she was already feeling.

She watched as Iversen made his way back to the car. He had just dropped her off after a trip to the local store for some essentials. He had offered to do the shopping for her, but she had insisted on going. She didn't explain why; she needed some items that would raise questions, and she wasn't ready to answer any of them just yet. Hell, maybe she would never be ready, but this way, she would at least avoid them for a little longer.

The teakettle in the kitchen started whistling, and she poured the boiling water into a mug. The choice of tea didn't matter; she just needed something. Tea usually ran through her like water through a pipe, and that was exactly what she needed right now. She placed herself at the counter and started sipping from the cup, not bothering with letting it cool first and accepting her fate after having burned her tongue.

After finishing, she placed the mug down and stared at it, waiting for her brain to register the empty mug so her bladder could start complaining, and she would have to pee. She waited and waited, but nothing happened. The water in the kettle was still warm, so she poured herself another cup and downed it quicker than the first one. Again, she waited, and again, nothing happened. Of course, this would be the one time where her body would absorb the liquid. The one time she needed it to act normal, was the one time it didn't.

She had almost given up when she got out of her seat and went to clean the mug. The sound of the tap seemed to trigger her bladder, and she hurried to the bathroom, almost forgetting the thing she needed and the whole reason for doing this in the first place.

All that was left now was the endless wait. She set an alarm and started pacing the floor of the bathroom. It wasn't a big room, so she mostly just walked in circles. She was rubbing her palms together and started walking quicker. At times, she swore it was like she just teleported from one spot in the bathroom to another.

Pacing, waiting, fidgeting.

Then the alarm went off. She almost pushed her phone into the toilet by the sudden move to switch it off but managed to catch it on the edge and wiped it down before turning to the plastic stick on the counter. She looked at it, and her heart sank.

She should have known. She had known. She did know. All the signs were there. She suspected it; why else would she take the test? *Oh, God! No, no, no, no, no.* She started pacing again, closed her eyes, and then looked at the stick again. Same result. *Why, God, why?* she thought to herself, not wanting to acknowledge the truth. Nevertheless, it was real; seeing it now made it real. At the same time, it made it hurt. Of course, it would go like this. Nothing ever went her way. All odds were stacked against her from the moment her dad had taken his eyes off her all those years ago. Ever since the kidnapping, hell, maybe even since her birth. Repeatedly the universe had proven that it was mighty, and she was merely a human, fragile, and without any say in this life.

Her hand clenched the plastic stick as she slid down the wall. She regretted looking at it, taking it, buying it. She knew ignoring it didn't make it any less real; it would just make her less prepared.

She couldn't be pregnant. She couldn't; it just couldn't be true.

But she was pregnant, and she had not needed a test to confirm that. She had lost count of when her last period was, and she had seen the changes to her body. If she had to guess, she would say that she was about fourteen weeks pregnant. It would match with the last couple of days with Nate, unless it was from that one-night stand a while back. Either way, it was definitely inconvenient.

She didn't show much; her stomach was hard and looked bloated but not excessively. She didn't think anyone else had noticed. She had been eating more lately and naturally gaining weight, so it hadn't been unnatural for her body to change like this.

The full extent of what the plastic stick confirmed began to settle in. The thought had tugged at her for months, always lingering in the back of her head, but she had chosen to ignore it, to push it away until it was a better time to let it settle in. Though it would never be the right time. Now, had just been a terrible day so she had figured, why not make it worse?

She sighed and rested the back of her head against the wall. Tears were escaping and running down her cheeks.

"Pull yourself together, Hemmer," she whispered to herself and looked down at the stick she had never expected to hold. She had always found women more attractive, so being in a situation like this was never something she had imagined. The last time she had been holding a pregnancy test, it had not been her own; it had been Andrea's, and they had gone through it all together. This time it was just her; she was alone.

Alone and pregnant.

Her first sobs were strangled and breathless, but before long, she was full-out wailing. She curled up on the tiles and tried to make herself as small as possible so the universe would not see her, maybe give her some peace. But the universe did see her. No matter how small she made herself, she would always have a target on her back, and the universe would not give up its claws in her.

With loneliness came guilt, and as she was curled up on the floor trying to become invisible to the world, she suddenly felt responsible for it all, felt the weight of the world come crashing on top of her. Screaming, she felt her bones break and her breath being ripped away.

All those women. All those lives.

Mothers, sisters, daughters.

She curled into herself further, hugged her arms tightly around her knees, and dug fingernails into the skin there. Her screams had died, now the shaking started, and she felt herself drenched in sweat. The pressure still heavy on her and the pain still crawling its way through her body.

Alone. Unwanted. Unloved. Worthless.

Her fingers became numb, and her teeth started rattling. Tears were still falling. She kept her eyes closed tight. Mumbled the words she kept hearing.

"You are alone, you are unwanted, nobody loves you, you are worthless." All the while she was seeing all the dead bodies being dumped around her like trash. Women who all looked like her. Women who had their lives taken because of her. Humans killed for sport. People murdered in the search for her.

Another body fell. She rolled over the others and landed on her side, looking directly into Linda's eyes, staring with cold eyes through her soul, and Linda blamed herself for it all.

"Trish?" she whispered with a broken voice and reached for her sister. With hands shaking, she ghosted Trish's skin and the second it made contact, her sister turned into dirt. One by one, they turned to compost, and soil started filling the room, burying Linda underneath it all, suffocating her, as she was curled up on the bathroom floor.

Slowly the dirt disappeared. The suffocation ended, and the pressure on her body released. The pain through her body let go, and she could breathe again.

She was alive. She survived, and they all died.

She took a breath and dried her tears, the words from before still replaying in her mind.

Alone. Unwanted. Unloved. Worthless.

CHAPTER 26

Andrea had just finished a long shift. Her body was aching to rest in bed with a cup of tea and a good book. She sat in her car, felt her eyelids grow heavy, and found no relief from the coffee she sipped. *Immune to caffeine*, she thought to herself and took another sip. At least the taste was still there, and her body seemed to react to that. Caffeine or not, her body knew that when those delicious drops hit her lips, it was wake-up time. She closed her eyes and enjoyed a quiet moment while she let that taste reach every part of her mouth.

She was startled when her phone rang.

"Hello? Oh, Arnold, hi, how is everything?" she asked with a chipper tone. "No, I have not heard from her, but I am headed over there now. I know she needs space from me, but I would rather go there and show her support for her to kick me out, than not show up and her thinking we have abandoned her."

Arnold agreed with that and asked for an update once she got there. Andrea finished the last of her coffee and headed off. She tried phoning Linda a few times on her way, but the call went straight to voicemail.

It was not unusual for Linda to not answer her phone, but it still left an unsettling feeling in Andrea's stomach, and she may have driven a bit faster than the speed limits permitted.

The police car was still parked outside, and she gave a small wave to Iversen. He reluctantly waved back and didn't seem all that pleased to see her. Andrea had eyes and could see Iversen's infatuation with Linda, and she understood it. She of all people was not one to judge, seeing as she too was still in love with her ex-wife, but she didn't like the attention Iversen was giving her. It was clear he had a crush, but he was creepy about it. Andrea had caught him staring many times and not just a regular stare.

He had looked at Linda with hunger and longing, like she had once been his but no longer was.

She had discussed it with Annalise one night, and Annelise had noticed the same, but Arnold had assured them that was just how Iversen looked at women, which really didn't make it any less unsettling. Nevertheless, he cared for Linda, and Andrea hoped that meant he would do anything to protect her. And that was all she could ask for. The more people who cared for Linda, the safer she was.

No one answered her knocking on the door, and after attempting to call Linda a few times, Andrea pulled out her spare key and opened the front door. The house was dead quiet. Maybe Linda was sleeping. Andrea hoped she was sleeping, but a nervous feeling settled in her gut.

"Linda?" She called out and then closed the front door, making sure to lock it, so she wouldn't find Mr. Creep Iversen walking in on her. "Linda," she called again, louder this time. Her voice echoed through the hallway, but no response came.

A letter was addressed to her on the kitchen counter. *Andrea,* it said; she recognised Linda's handwriting. "Linda," she called again, this time more urgently. She clung the letter to her chest and ran through the house, opened every door, and looked everywhere. Linda was nowhere to be found.

She called her phone and heard it ringing from the bathroom. She found it on the floor next to a positive pregnancy test, and for a second, all colour drained from her face. *Linda is pregnant? How is she pregnant?* Her mind was racing, then she thought of Iversen, and she wanted to strangle him.

She grabbed her phone, called Arnold, and explained the situation, and soon both he and Annelise were on their way.

Outside, they had had a shift change. Iversen and his partner had left, and in their place were two other officers. Andrea approached them and explained that Linda was missing. Soon the whole force was there, and everyone was looking for her.

Andrea retracted into Willa's room and curled up on her bed. The sheets still smelled like her little girl, and everything looked as it had that day. Linda had done a great job in keeping everything intact. Looking around, it was like Willa was still there. "Please look out for your mommy, little one. Please keep her safe, please." She felt her eyes grow heavy with tears. She went to wipe them away when she felt the letter that she had still clenched in her hand.

With shaky hands, she carefully straightened the envelope and opened it. Linda's handwriting was everywhere, and dried tears covered the pages. Andrea's heart started beating in her chest, and she felt a growing anxiety raising from her gut.

Dear Andrea,

> I am sorry. I think you know why, but I couldn't find another way. There was no other way. The pain was simply getting too much. I am sorry …

"No," Andrea shouted and tossed the letter across the room. "No, you do not get to do this. No!" She stormed out of the room and ran outside to the others. "Arnold! She- she … she …"

"Breathe, Andrea, breathe. Slow breaths. We will find her. Just breathe." Arnold spoke slowly and wrapped his arms around the shaking woman.

"No, no, she— she did this. She wrote me a letter." She felt the arms around her release a bit till she met the old man's kind and worried eyes. "Arnold, she is going to kill herself."

Silence echoed among them all. Only Andrea's sobs cut through the void. Realising what had happened, saying it out loud, it became too much for Andrea, and she collapsed in Arnold's arms, clung to him like her life depended on it. Annelise was the first one to move. She took Arnold's place and guided Andrea inside.

"Find her," she whispered to her husband. Arnold nodded with a determined look, and suddenly everyone was moving around like a coordinated attack.

They were going to find Linda. They had to find her; they had to.

Inside, Annelise had put on some water for tea, while Andrea once again was curled up in Willa's bed. Her eyes were locked on the letter she had thrown across the room. She wanted to scream. She wanted to cry. She wanted to yell or punch something. How had she missed this? How had it gotten this bad without anyone knowing?

"Andrea, darling," Annelise called.

"In here," Andrea called back and saw the small woman appear in the doorway.

"What are you doing in here?" Andrea shook her shoulders and made room for Annelise to sit on the bed. "Is that the letter over there?"

"Yeah."

"Have you read it?"

"No, I don't think I can."

Annelise picked up the papers, folded them neatly, and placed them on the bed. "Do you think it was this bad before she got back?"

"What do you mean?" Annelise asked.

"What if she has been feeling like this for years but only held it together for Tucker? What if losing him was what sent her over the edge, gave her permission to give up?"

Annelise hummed again and was quite for a long time, chewing on the words Andrea had shared.

She began, "I think that is very likely. Linda has never had it easy, and I have been fearing this day ever since you two lost little Willa. I think she has needed help that no one has been able to give her. Instead of coping, she threw herself into work, did everything in her power to help others, while she didn't give herself the time of day. Losing her grandmother broke her heart, but losing Trish, and losing her like that, it must have ripped out her heart completely. She started therapy, but I don't think she even realised how much it all had affected her. Then seeing all those women murdered by the same person who kidnapped and tortured her as a child, it cannot have been easy. Losing Tucker was a great loss, yes, but it was just a small piece in the grand scheme of things. I think you are right that she was only holding it together for him. Now with him gone, she thinks she has nothing left to fight for. But she is wrong. She has everything to fight for; she just needs to choose to see it. We are right here. We are all right here, and we love her so much." Andrea cried and felt the old woman wrap her up in a warm hug.

They sat like that for a while, holding each other and praying for Linda. They were both going to have some stern words with her once they got her back.

"She is pregnant," Andrea whispered, and Annelise looked at her with wide eyes.

"She told you this?"

"No, I was calling her phone and could hear it ringing from the bathroom. I found it on the floor next to a positive pregnancy test." Andrea studied the older woman as she was taking in the words. "Do you, do you think she and Iversen have—"

"No," Annelise interrupted her. "No, don't even go there."

Andrea nodded and accepted the tea that was handed to her. "Drink this and read this. Then come join me in the kitchen. I am sure the others will have some news by then."

Andrea nodded again and sighed when she heard the door close.

"What have you done, Linda? What have you done?" she whispered and reached for the letter.

Dear Andrea,

> I am sorry. I think you know why, but I couldn't find another way. There was no other way. The pain was simply getting too much. I am sorry that I am such a coward, but I know you will be better off without me. The world will be a better place. No more women will get murdered because of me. There will be no more killing, and everyone get to live in peace.
>
> Please know that I have had a good life. A happy life. Especially thanks to you.
>
> I am sorry, I am crying all over the paper, but I am not starting over again. This is already the fifth try; you can find the previous four attempts in the trash. If I continue like this, I will end up by taking a whole forest down with me.
>
> I can hear you laughing. Bet you didn't think this letter was going to make you laugh.
>
> I love your laugh. I love you.
>
> Did you know I always get butterflies whenever I see you?

The first time it happened, I stopped dead in my tracks. My entire nervous system short-circuited, and the neurons firing in my brain could not move my muscles. I remained frozen with my heart beating like a hundred drums that could probably be heard from outer space.

You, Miss Andrea Williams, you naturally exude sensuality and class, and you have an irresistible magnetism over you without even trying. Most people are pulled towards you, and I imagine it's difficult for you to walk anywhere without being eyed up by strangers.

Others are repelled by your success or intimidated by your beauty.

A conscious Miss Williams can be daunting and cold.

But a sleeping Miss Williams?

Well, a sleeping Miss Williams is the complete opposite, and I was sure the sight in front of me was going to cause my premature death. A sleeping Miss Williams is all things adorable and soft. The Ice Queen's poker face was gone and replaced with an innocent smile and delicate features. Your pale skin was washed by the moonlight that fell gently on your face. But the best of it all, what truly made you human and adorable, were the little snores you made in your sleep.

The second time was when you were making me breakfast a couple of weeks later. I couldn't help but feel that the Miss Williams standing in my kitchen flipping pancakes was the real deal. The one I had never been allowed to see before. This was the real you, Andrea. Beautiful.

The tall Ice Queen had melted.

With your heels off, you went from five feet six to five feet four, and after peeling back the layers of tailored suits and designer dresses, you were more of a comfort dresser. Baggy trousers and oversized shirts. Even your hair seemed relaxed, gathered in a loose bun, and your face completely without makeup.

I felt privileged that I was allowed to see this beautiful woman, to see you with your guard down.

I remember walking around the kitchen island and carefully stepping behind you, wrapping my arms around your waist. You smelled so nice. A scent I since came to learn was your flowery scented shampoo.

I liked it when you let me hold you like that.

I knew I loved you then.

I love you still.

I hope you find your peace.

I hope you find love.

You deserve it all and more.

Goodbye, my love.
Yours always, Linda

CHAPTER 27

The stiff wind hit Linda's cheek as she stepped out on the ledge, and she almost lost her footing. She should have felt the urge to wrap her arms around herself or tremble from the cold. Instead, she felt nothing, not even the goosebumps tightening over her skin. An involuntary shiver ran through her body, but she barely noticed it.

The wind howled around her, making it hard to hear the water running below her. Her hair fell out of its loose bun and danced around her face, the wind tugging at it without mercy.

Unsteady feet ghosted their way along the ledge till she reached the opening between the barriers. The wind hit her hard, and she nearly lost her balance. By instinct, she reached out for the railing and grabbed the metal tightly, releasing a jagged breath. That had been close. Part of her regretted having saved herself. It would have been easier to get pushed off by the wind rather than jumping.

She forced another breath out, willing her stomach to stop twisting itself and keep the liquor down. She leaned forward and stared into the water. The surface was black and almost looked like a street, and she wondered how her body would break once it made contact with it. Deep down, she knew she wasn't up high enough to make a real impact. She would most like survive the fall, but she hoped the cold water in combination with the drugs and alcohol would knock her out, and the water would wash her away.

She closed her eyes and searched for a memory that she could find peace in, something that would make her heart full and spread one last smile on her face.

She knew just the memory, her go-to memory when things seemed too dark to handle.

Angela was lying in the hospital bed, clinging to Linda's hand for dear life. Sweat was running off her forehead, and red patches of heat had appeared on her pale skin. She groaned loudly in discomfort as another wave of pain surged through her body. Gritting her teeth, she tightened her grip around Linda's hand.

"Breathe, love, just breathe," Linda said and wiped her forehead with a cloth, a mixture of nerves and anticipation in her voice about what was about to happen.

"Fuck, I can't focus on breathing exercises, Linda. I am having a fucking baby," Andrea growled as the contraction reached its peak.

She had been in labour for eight hours now, and the contractions were getting closer and closer, growing in intensity each time. Linda smiled and kissed her cheek.

"I know, love, but I need you to breathe for me, please? Our little girl is not out yet, and she needs oxygen, and so do you. I can't have you pass out on me, so I need you to breathe for me, please."

"I hate you," Andrea mumbled and received another kiss.

"I know. Now take a deep breath for me."

Andrea reluctantly closed her eyes and took a deep breath. "Another. And one more." Slowly her shoulders started to relax, and she felt the tension in her lower back ease a little. She opened her eyes and looked to her wife.

"Okay that helped a little, but I still hate you." Andrea mumbled with a smile and kept taking deep breaths.

The door opened, and Dr. Jones came in and approached the bed.

"Andrea, Linda. How are things going in here? How far apart are the contractions?"

"A little under a minute," Linda replied. She had been keeping a close watch on them.

"Alright, very good. Andrea, I'm just going to take a quick look to see how dilated you are." Dr. Jones smiled reassuringly as he put on a pair of gloves and carefully felt around for a minute before withdrawing his hand. "Okay, everything looks good. You are fully dilated, and we can get started. That is, if you are ready to meet your baby girl?"

"So ready," Linda and Andrea replied in unison.

A few minutes later, it was time to push. Linda had never been in such awe of her wife before, of the female body in general. What a beautiful thing the body could do.

"It fucking hurts," Andrea shrieked between breaths.

"You are doing so great. Just a little more, love," Linda said soothingly and stroked her hair.

"Fine, but if we are having another one, then you are doing this next time, and I will be on the sideline, cheering you on," Andrea yelled, trying to control her breath before the next push.

Linda chuckled quietly, looked at her wife, and didn't think she could love anyone more than her.

Seven pushes in, and Andrea was exhausted. An excruciating contraction had just subsided, and another was quickly building.

"I can see the head," Linda cried," and Andrea smiled. *Dear Lord, that really is like pushing a watermelon through a doughnut,* Linda thought to herself.

"Linda," Andrea panted.

"Yeah?" Linda asked nervously and grabbed her hand. She could see the pain in every part of Andrea's face, mixed with other emotions she couldn't quite decipher.

"Not helping," Andrea shouted.

"What?"

"I do not need to think of watermelons and doughnut holes right now," Andrea managed to get out before she felt another contraction build.

"Shit, I said that out loud?" The look on Andrea's face was answer enough. "Sorry."

She gripped Linda's hand so tight she feared for a moment it might break, but she ignored it and focused on Andrea as she pushed and screamed. She was clearly drained for energy but kept going. Kept pushing, and all of a sudden, they could hear crying.

Andrea fell back on the bed, breathing heavily, and closed her eyes for a brief second, trying to gain some strength before opening them again and looking at Linda. She tried to get eye contact, but Linda's gaze was fixed on something at the end of the bed.

There was a little human.

"You did it, love." Linda smiled widely and gave her wife a kiss.

Andrea feared that the smile would split her wife's face in two. The love radiating from that smile was all the strength she needed to stay awake for a little longer.

"I'm so proud of you; I love you so much."

A young nurse approached the bed, holding a light pink bundle in her arms. She carefully handed the bundle over to Andrea and gave her a bright smile.

Seeing Andrea hold their child for the first time, all sweaty and tired; that was Linda's happiest memory. It filled her chest with warmth and love, and she wanted to stay in that memory forever.

A gust of wind sent shivers down her spine and brought her back to reality. Her eyes snapped open, and the heat in her chest quickly died as she was once again overcome by emptiness. She was alone, and the happy memories were no longer enough to comfort her. Tears obscured her vision, making the moonlight fuzzy and reflected in every tear. One after the other, they glided over her cheeks, stopping briefly at her chin before plummeting towards the dark water below. As she silently wept, she removed her hands from the railing, steadying herself and desperately clutching at her chest. A ragged breath left her lungs, almost suppressed by the sheer pressure her sobs were putting on her lungs.

The emptiness was so overbearing, so heavy, so painful that in one last attempt, she wanted to reach in and fill that void that consumed her chest. Eyes screwed shut, wanting so badly to block out the pain.

Alone. Unwanted. Unloved. Worthless.

Her sobs were now audible. Her legs were shaking as she opened her eyes. Determined.

Shifting her footing just a little bit, she again closed her eyes and leaned forward.

CHAPTER 28

"Linda!" What sounded like Andrea's voice cut through the wind like a newly sharpened blade. Linda remained on the ledge, her eyes searching for her ex-wife. "Linda," a voice called again, this time deeper and more rusty. "Linda!"

Arnold came running down the bridge and pulled her back to safety.

"You crazy girl," he yelled and took off his jacket to wrap her in it. "What were you thinking?" His hands were shaking, and he was out of breath. Linda remembered his heart condition and forgot about herself completely.

"Are you okay? Do you have any chest pain?" she asked and started examining him like he had been the one about to fall to his death.

"Am I alright? Jesus, woman, you scared the life out of all of us, so no. No, I am not alright." He was still yelling, and his pulse was racing.

"You should take a deep breath, maybe sit down, catch your breath?"

"Don't you tell me to calm down. I almost lost you," he shouted, grabbing her by the shoulders. "Don't you ever do anything like this again, do you hear me?"

Linda nodded repeatedly, not realising she had caused everyone so much pain.

Arnold took a breath and continued, more calmly now, "You are so loved. So many people love you so much. And we simply cannot imagine a world without you; do you understand?" Linda nodded again. "We need you. Your parents, they just lost your sister; they can't lose you too. Your brother and sister, your nieces and nephews, it would break their hearts, and they have already been through enough." He took another breath and wrapped her up in his arms. "Annelise and I, damn it, Linda, we love you.

You are like a daughter to us. Losing you would not just break our hearts, it would rip them from our chests completely."

"I'm sorry. I'm sorry. I'm so sorry," Linda sobbed, and Arnold tightened his hold on her.

"Nothing to apologise for; just know that you are so loved, my child, and we would be devastated if you weren't here."

They stood like that for a while, comforting each other. Then Linda started shaking. The cold had gotten to her, and she became groggy from all the medication she had taken prior to going there. She was in an ambulance before she was fully out of it, and not once did Arnold let go of her hand.

She wasn't alone. She wasn't alone at all.

A quiet buzzing of voices sounded around her as she came to. Doctors had already checked her out the last time she woke up. This time, she was surrounded by family. The warm feeling from before spread through her and tugged kindly at her heart.

She wasn't alone.

"Uno," a child's voice called out. Linda recognised it as her nephew, Liam. From the sounds of their discussions, he seemed to be on a winning streak that his older brother did not approve of. Linda laughed quietly at them. Suddenly, the whole room went quiet, and everyone's eyes turned to Linda in the bed.

"Aunty?" Liam asked curiously and crawled up in the bed.

"Linda?" her mother called. She started crying at the sound of a hoarse "Hey" from Linda, and soon after, they were all hugging her and telling her how loved she was. Some were crying; some were laughing. Her sister was yelling, and her father didn't say much.

"You had us terrified," her brother said, kissing her cheek.

"I'm sorry," Linda whispered and felt streaming from her eyes.

"Don't apologise; just please promise me you will talk to someone next time, yeah?" her brother begged, and Linda nodded.

"Next time!" Helen erupted. "There won't be a next time, will there, Linda?" She was angry; it was understandable, normal even. "Let me put it like this: 1If you ever, *ever* pull anything like this again, I will kill you myself."

"Helen," their mother interjected.

Her sister was about to apologise when Linda started laughing. She was laughing so much her cheeks started hurting. A heart-warming and contagious laughter soon filled the room, and everyone was laughing without really knowing why.

"What is happening here?" Arnold asked as he and Annelise entered the room. Linda quieted her laugh with a few soft chuckles and smiled lovingly at the elder couple.

"Thank you for saving me again," she said and reached for Arnold's hand.

He stepped closer, and the scent of firewood and sweet apple entered her nostrils. He had been smoking again. Linda smiled, imagining how Annelise had reacted to finding him puffing his pipe outside the hospital. Personally, she hoped he would never stop. There was something soothing and calming about the pipe, and it just fit his whole demeanour.

"Anything for you," he said sincerely.

Annelise squeezed her way past him and almost threw herself on the bed to hug Linda tightly.

"You had us all so worried, darling," she cried.

Linda wrapped her arms around her, and they hugged for a long time.

"I am so glad you are okay. My heart would have burst if we had lost you."

She kissed Linda's forehead and looked into her eyes for a long time before she got up, dragging Arnold along with her. She had insisted on him getting a checkup after this stressful day. She didn't have energy to worry about his heart on top of everything else. For once, Arnold had not complained or tried to get around it. Today had been scary, and he figured it best to get the all-clear.

It was getting late, and one by one, they said their goodbyes and promised to do something together soon. They needed a family day, a whole day where they could play games, build forts, go hiking, and eat delicious food. Reconnect as a family. Linda like the sound of that, and she knew Trish would have loved it too.

Soon, it was just Linda and her parents in the room.

Her mother gave her husband a push and excused herself, said she would go to get some coffee, and left the room. Now it was just Linda and her father. They hadn't been alone in a room together since she was a child, before the kidnapping, before everything went wrong.

Her father was looking out the window. The lights from outside shone on his face, and Linda could see a tear slowly descending over his cheek. She hadn't seen him cry before, never seen him show any emotions.

"I am sorry," he said.

Linda almost fell out of the bed at the sound of his voice. It just now hit her that she hadn't heard him speak in years. She had entirely forgotten how his voice sounded.

He looked at her and walked towards her bed, sat down, and folded his hands awkwardly in his lap. "I am sorry," he repeated. "I don't think I've ever said that to you. I realise we never had a conversation after it all happened. We never talked about it. You didn't bring it up, and I didn't know what to say. The thing is, though, you were a child. It wasn't your responsibility to start that conversation. It was mine, and I didn't. I am sorry for that. Maybe a lot of this could have been prevented if we had just talked. Maybe I would have been able to protect you if I had just listened and given you more attention. That is a cross I will always have to bear. I cannot change what has happened, but I can promise to do better moving forward."

He was shaking, and Linda reached for his hand, a gesture so unusual for them to share, yet it felt normal. Right.

"It's okay, Dad."

Her father shook his head.

"No, it is not. I have already lost one daughter; I will not lose another. I will not lose you. I am sorry, if I was part of creating an environment where you did not feel loved. If I did that, then I failed as a father, because you are loved, Linda, my sweet girl. You fill my heart. I love you so much, and I am so immensely proud of you. You have a fire inside of you, a bravery I have not seen like it in anyone else. Please don't ever give up, because if anyone deserves happiness, it is you, my daughter."

They shared a smiled and held each other's hands for a bit. They thought about hugging, but neither seemed ready to take that step just yet, though this was a huge step in the right direction.

Their moment was interrupted by the sound of clicking heels from the hallway. Her father chuckled softly and gave her hands a final squeeze. "Sounds like your wife is here."

"Ex-wife," Linda corrected him.

"I know, but maybe you should change that. I realise I haven't always been your greatest supporter, but that woman loves you. That much I can see, and I think you love her too. What you two have is rare; don't let it go to waste." He walked towards to door.

"Hey, Dad," Linda called after him, as Andrea entered the room. "I love you too."

A smile spread on his face that she hadn't seen before. They shared a look, and he was gone.

Linda awoke a few hours later. Something heavy was pressing against her side, and she could smell a familiar flowery shampoo. Opening her eyes, she saw ebony-coloured hair sprawled out over her chest and heard the familiar soft snores from her ex-wife. Andrea had curled up in the bed next to her, cuddling her side like she was her favourite pillow. Linda smiled and hugged her closer.

It was dark outside. Visiting hours were probably over a long time ago, but she could imagine Andrea threatening to sue the hospital if she wasn't allowed to stay.

Her snores became muffled as she buried her face in the crook of Linda's neck. Her breath tickled, and Linda couldn't help but feel warm at the touch.

She had been so wrong, standing on the ledge. Making the decision to end it all had been so wrong.

She was still carrying the guilt, still feeling the pain, but it felt lighter now. It was like all the love helped her carry it all. She would be okay. It would all be okay.

"I can hear you thinking," Andrea mumbled into her neck, and Linda smiled. She felt a brief peck to the skin there before Andrea retracted herself, looked her in the eyes, and asked, "Tell me, what is going on in that head of yours?" Andrea pushed her body flushed with Linda's.

"I was just thinking how lucky I am," Linda answered and took a leap of faith. She leaned forward and connected their lips in a brief kiss. "Was that okay?"

Andrea answered by capturing her lips again, sighing contently as she deepened the kiss.

"It is very okay." She smiled and curled back up in the nape of her neck.

Linda stared into the ceiling, feeling her ex-wife's breath get slow and even. She was about to fall back asleep. She had to say this, had to say it now before she lost her confidence.

"I- I—" She took a breath. "I am not good at saying, 'I love you.' But I do," Linda whispered in the dark, worrying that Andrea might not know.

Andrea smiled and tugged her closer, brushing her lips over her neck in a soft peck.

"When it comes to love, I think that words are supposed to be affirmations of what is already real and known. They are not the substance. They are just an added affection. They are supposed to reference something that is far more than just words. I think love itself is always an action." She briefly kissed Linda's cheek and then moved to look her in the eyes. "I know and feel that I am loved by you all the time. No absence of words could ever take any of that away from me. I have always felt loved by you." She watched as Linda's eyes grew heavy, and she held her gaze. Smiled at her warmly before she leaned in and kissed her. "And I love you too, Linda. Of course, I love you."

Linda chuckled and sighed contently.

She had never felt safer than right this second.

CHAPTER 29

"Fffff fff fff fff, ff-fff fff fffff fff ff-fff." Whistling echoed through the halls of the abandoned building, the sound fighting for dominance with the wind and the creaking structure. Stray cats were fighting nearby, and their cries carried with the echo, traveling further than the light could reach.

Downstairs in the basement was no light, and no echo travelled this far. Only small sobs and shivers could be heard from the far corner of the basement. In that corner was a little girl, shivering from the cold. She was sitting on her knees, rocking back and forth, with her hands tapping at the brick wall. She was crying and sniffling in the dark. The back of her dress had been ripped open, and blood was running down her back.

The whistling came closer, and the sound of a door opening made the little girl stop her movements. A young boy walked in and quieted his whistling as he approached the girl.

"Linda?" he whispered. The girl turned her head and looked at him with teary eyes. "I brought you soup," the boy said and placed a bowl on the floor, a bit out of her reach. "Why are you crying?"

"Hurts," Linda replied shortly and reached for the soup.

It had been a long time since she had eaten, so the soup was gone quickly. She withdrew into the corner, as the boy moved closer. Her eyelids felt heavy, and soon after, she could feel herself being positioned on the floor, facing down. The cold concrete gave her shivers, and she wanted to get back up. She asked the boy to help her, but soon after, she fell asleep and forgot about it completely.

The boy was standing over her sleeping body with a wide grin on his face. He switched on the lights and admired the work he had done. Her back was still uncovered, and once he started washing the blood away, he could really see the result of his work. All over her back were deep lines cut into her skin. The lines went from the back of her neck down her spine and over her hips. They then made a wing formation, going back up her body to the shoulder blades and connecting back to her neck. This was on both sides.

This was merely the outline of what was going to be his masterpiece.

He sharpened his knife and sat down atop of her, wondered for a second where to start, and then put the blade to her skin. It cut easily and deep. Fresh blood released from the immediate touch, and a new excited smile spread across his face.

He took his time. Made sure, he repeated his movements on both sides, making it symmetrical and beautiful. The carvings started to take shape, looking like feathers carved into her back as a set of wings.

"My angel," he whispered and kept cutting.

He thought he would never stop.

It wasn't until she started to come to that he quickly cleaned up and excited the room. Leaving her alone in the darkness once again.

Linda felt a shiver down her body as the nightmare faded away, and she started to wake up. She was afraid to open her eyes, fearful that she would be back in that place, that her whole life up until this point had been a dream, and she had been stuck there all along.

A quiet snore sounded near her ear, and she felt a breath against her neck. *Andrea*, she thought and felt relief wash over her. It wasn't a dream. Her life was real. She was safe.

She hugged Andrea closer and felt comfortable enough to close her eyes again. The warmth the two of them shared made her relax, and she was asleep again not long after.

> "It is okay; it's okay," the boy said with a soothing voice and hugged her. "The bad man has gone now."
>
> Linda shivered and clung to him.
>
> "You are my only friend," she whispered. "Please don't leave me."
>
> "You are my only friend too, and I will never leave you. We will always be together," he promised and squeezed her tight.
>
> "You promise?" Linda asked and looked in his eyes.
>
> "I promise," he said and lifted his pinkie.
>
> "A pinkie-promise." Linda beamed and suddenly felt like they could conquer it all. As long as they were together, the bad man couldn't get to them.

"Jasper," Linda gasped, as she woke again.

It was still night-time, and the room was lit in a dim blue light. She released a breath and checked to make sure she hadn't woken up Andrea. She shifted in the bed and carefully untangled herself from the woman sleeping beside her. Wires were entangled everywhere, and it turned out to be quite the maze before she got free.

She walked to the bathroom and stood by the sink for a bit. The water running from the tap, as she just stared at it. She had remembered something during the nightmare; it was what had woken her up, but now she couldn't recall what it was.

"Come on, Hemmer, think. Think," she whispered to herself and rubbed her head. *Jasper*, she thought again and sat down on the floor. *Why does that name sound familiar?* She leaned her head back and carefully banged it into the wall behind her. "Think, Hemmer, think. Who is

Jasper?" She went back in time, figured it was one of Nate's associates, but what would the chances be of that?

Then a memory flashed before her; she initially pushed it away because it was uncomfortable, but it kept coming back to her. It was insistent.

She had just said goodbye to Tucker and watched him ride off when Iversen came by.

He had shown up out of the blue and asked her for dinner, and before she had been given a chance to answer, he had asked her if she wanted to know his first name now that they would be dating. She had been quite taken aback by that, as she had never once initiated anything with him. Maybe the shock of all that information had block out the next part.

Before she knew it, they were kissing. He kissed her, and then he got upset when she turned him down. The whole thing had sent her into a panic attack, and she had had to call Arnold to calm her down.

Why am I thinking of this? Why is this significant?

She went through it again, step by step. From the moment Iversen arrived, till the moment she kicked him out. Some part of her brain told her that this was the missing piece, that this was the memory she had to decipher, that this was important. She just couldn't remember why. *Why? Why is this important?*

Her brain told her she was getting closer. It was right there, but still not really. It was like knowing the answer to a question and knowing that you knew, but just not being able to formulate it or have that memory just out of reach. It was right on the tip of her tongue, but what was it?

"He arrived. He asked me out. He told me his name. He kissed me, and I kicked him out." She listed the events and went through them slowly. "He arrived. He asked me out. He told me his name. He kissed me, and I kicked him out." She repeated it over and over. Kept banging her head against the wall, going over the events again and again. "He arrived. He asked me out ..."

She stopped.

It finally clicked.

Her eyes went wide, and her body started shaking involuntarily. She was having a panic attack, one she did not have the energy or time for. *He told me his name*, she thought and curled up on the floor. The shaking increased, and the tears started clouding her vision. *Jasper! It is Jasper. Iversen is Jasper.*

The bathroom door was opened, and Andrea quickly got down on her knees beside Linda. She shouted for help, not caring about the other patients sound asleep.

Linda looked at her and tried to speak, but Andrea just shushed her and asked her to breathe.

The nurse came, and then Linda passed out from a lack of oxygen; she was given a sedative to help her relax. Clearly, she had some traumas from the events of the night that were wearing her down. They would deal with them later. For now, she just needed to sleep.

CHAPTER 30

Andrea was called to work early that morning. Her phone woke her from her sleep, and she grabbed it so quickly, she almost fell out of bed. Linda instinctively reached for her in her sleep, and Andrea had considered getting back in bed, curling up next to her ex-wife. But her colleague on the phone was insisting, and she had been out of the office for a few days now. Maybe if she was quick about it, she could return at noon and take Linda for lunch.

She took one last look at Linda and left to take care of work.

The events of last night replayed in Linda's mind. The nightmares, the memories, they all came to her at once, and she woke with a sudden gasp of air; she had to take a minute to steady herself. She felt a panic attack coming on but managed to catch it in time. She closed her eyes, slowed her breath, and thought of the last thing she had to eat, the last person she spoke with, the last colour she noticed, and the last smell she remembered. Focusing on these things allowed her to distract her brain from the anxiety and steady her heartbeat, one breath at a time.

She took another couple of deep breaths and looked around the room. The sun was up, and she could hear the quiet buzzing of people walking around the hospital. The side of the bed where Andrea had been sleeping was empty. She felt the sheets with her hand and found it cold. Maybe she had been asked to leave after the incident late last night. She looked to the nightstand and found a note with her name on it. At first, she thought Andrea had left her a note and found it cute. But it wasn't Andrea's handwriting, and the uncomfortable feeling in her stomach returned.

She unfolded the note and read.

My sweet angel,

    Since you are so very well protected with strong police officers and twenty-four-hour surveillance, it is difficult for me to get to you. Don't you see that? All I want is to be with you.

    We pinkie-promised that we would always be together, remember?

    Nevertheless, if you don't want me, then I will just have to find someone else, now won't I?

    The question is just who to choose?

    You do of course have another sister, and it would be fun to say that I got the full collection. But no … She looks like you, and I think I have grown tired of that model.

    No, I think I want to try something entirely different, maybe something with green eyes and ebony hair?

    Bet I got your attention now.

    I will be at our spot; you remember where it is, right?

    Come alone, and don't take too long!

Your maker

    Linda's hands started shaking. *He has Andrea? How can he have Andrea? She was just here.* Her mind was racing, and before she knew it, she was out of bed and putting on her clothes.

    She grabbed her phone and tried calling Andrea, hoping she would pick up and this had all been a scare game. She waited patiently while the phone rang. After the seventh ring, it went to voicemail. *Shit!* Linda cursed internally and tried again. After the fourth dial, she decided to leave a voicemail and maybe text her. Fifth dial happened, and she waited for the sound of Andrea's voice asking her to leave a voicemail, but the sound never came. She waited and waited, like time stood still, but there was no option given to leave a voicemail and no further dial tone was heard.

"Fuck," she cursed and looked at her phone to try and call again. She tapped frantically at the screen, but it didn't react at all. A wave of frustration went through her, as she realised its battery had run out.

Time was ticking fast, and if the Angel Maker really had Andrea, then there was no time to waste. She tossed the phone on the bed and continued getting dressed. *My shoes; where are my shoes?* she thought and went through all the cabinets looking for them. Her movements stilled as a nurse was making her way into her room. Linda quickly hid in the bathroom and to her delight saw that her shoes were on a shelf by the door.

The nurse left the room, and Linda made her way out of the hospital. The security detail outside her room was asleep, and she was able to sneak past them. No one stopped her. No one asked her any questions. She just got up and left.

Getting out of the hospital was easy enough. Getting to where she needed to be was going to be a challenge. She didn't have her wallet with her and no money in her pockets. The hospital was downtown, and she had at least a three-hour walk ahead of her. She couldn't remember the exact location of the forest, but it had to be in the case files somewhere.

She thought about going home and researching, but she couldn't waste the time. Moreover, her home was under surveillance, so they would probably see her and try to stop her, and that couldn't happen. Andrea's life was on the line, and Linda was not going to risk it. Especially not now. Besides, she didn't know who to trust anymore, knowing that Iversen had in fact been the perpetrator all along.

The forest was cold, just like it had been then, and the memories were overwhelming. She hadn't known where to go; still her body had led the way, and now she was definitely in the right place. Goosebumps spread on her entire body. Her muscles and limbs felt stiff, and she couldn't quite catch her breath. It was like something heavy hit her in the stomach, and she almost fell to her knees.

This was the forest; there was no doubt about it. It had to be. She had never been here herself, but Jasper had shown her videos of the place and described it in all of his stories. It was one of the things that had made her trust him: his storytelling. He had always made her feel better with one of his stories, giving her a glimpse into a magical place that seemed out of reach, a sense of freedom she never thought she would see again.

She found the main path.

"Enter the forest and turn right after three lines." *Three lines ... three lines of what? What had he said?* She closed her eyes and tried to remember.

> Linda had refused to eat, and the man keeping her had slapped her across the face. Jasper had been there for her and comforted her, held her and told her they would always be friends.
>
> "If we ever get lost from each other, then you can always find me in the Garden of Eden," Jasper said and hugged her, getting excited to feel her wings against the palm of his hands. "Only angels are allowed in the Garden of Eden."
>
> "But Jasper, I am not an angel. Am I?"
>
> "Yes, you are, my angel. You even have wings," he said and showed her back in the mirror. "See, you have wings. You are an angel, and all angels have wings."
>
> "So I can get into the garden?" Linda asked, and Jasper nodded.
>
> "Yes, you can. You just have to remember the way." Having a place where they could be together and be safe sounded calming and comfortable, and that was exactly what Linda needed. She wanted to know where this place was; she wanted to know where to find her friend, should they ever get lost from each other.
>
> "How do I find it?" she asked.
>
> "You find the entrance to the forest and go straight. Turn right after three lines."

She remembered his melody and started walking. "Fffff fff fff fff, ff-fff fff fffff fff ff-fff." She never thought that her friend had been the person doing all the bad things to her. She had trusted him completely. And after she was rescued, she never tried to find this place because she was told that Jasper never existed, that she had made him and all the stories up in her minds. That he was her fantasy-friend. Someone she had made up to keep herself safe and help her forget what was happening. She had just been a kid, and it had all made sense.

Now, thinking back, she got frustrated with the doctors and police for not believing her. If they had, they could have found this place a long time ago. Instead, over thirty women had to die before they found it. Over thirty lives had been lost that they could have prevented, had they just listened.

She stopped walking and then looked to her right. Yellow police markers were still stuck to the tree, and she knew she was headed in the right direction. She turned right and continued. "Walk straight for seven lines and look for a clearing. Even at night the moon will light up the ground." Luckily the skies were clear, and she could indeed spot the moon from up between the trees. "Fffff fff fff fff, ff-fff fff fffff fff ff-fff."

The forest quickly got dense, but there still seemed to be a small path, like some deer had walked there and kept it clear. Linda wondered how many times Jasper had gone there. It couldn't just have been the thirty-two times he had buried someone. The path here was way too worn for that.

She got a dreadful feeling, thinking he had gone here just to jerk off and admire his work.

The trees started to clear, and she saw the spot. Police tape was still set up to protect the graves. A chill ran down her spine at the sight, and she wondered which of the graves had been Trish's.

"I am sorry," she whispered to no one and walked under the tape.

"There you are. I was starting to wonder if you were even coming." A familiar voice spoke behind her.

Linda stopped dead in her tracks, and a tear rolled down her cheek. *Iversen*, she thought. It really was him.

She swallowed hard and turned around. "Surprise."

Iversen smiled and took a step closer. Linda had decided to not show fear, to not let herself be intimidated, but she couldn't help taking a step back as he approached her. It was just an instinct, like her body took over and decided to protect her.

"Jasper," she whispered, and the smile on Iversen's face grew wider.

"You remember me. I knew you would."

"They told me you didn't exist. In the therapy I had afterwards, they told me I had made you up."

"Well, you didn't. I am right here. I have always been right here, waiting for you here at our spot. Just like I promised."

He stepped closer again, and again Linda stepped back, kept the space between them.

"But you never showed up. Not once." The anger in him was starting to show, just like it had that day in the kitchen when she had turned him down. "So I had to find someone else. You have to understand, I never meant to kill anyone. They just weren't as strong as you. I took them, gave them wings, and made them fly, but they couldn't fly like you. Then I figured, maybe bringing them to heaven's door first, showing them the way, and then making them return, would help them fly. It was exciting. It became a drug." He walked closer still.

"Then why did you kill them?"

"I just brought them home. I drowned them, tried to bring them back, but they didn't want to return. They chose to stay in heaven. They are there now, waiting for us, waiting for us to join them." He reached up and touched her cheek.

The skin contact brough Linda back to reality, and she quickly stepped back away from him.

"Where is Andrea?" she asked and put her stoneface back on. She was no longer Linda. Her undercover persona was back in charge, and all the walls were being rebuilt. Iversen saw the shift and made a displeased face.

"Why? Why do you care about her?"

"Where is she?" she asked again.

This time, she was the one to step closer. *I can take him on, if I have to. I can*, she tried to convince herself and eyed him up. He looked strong. He was probably stronger than her, as she was still recovering from all the traumas in the past year, but she still saw herself with a good chance.

"Where is she!" This time it was not a question, and she was right in his face. Iversen sighed and stepped back, started walking around the graves with a grin on his face.

"You really should stop caring so much. You are already too late. I doubt she has any more air left." He looked at the ground below his feet. The snow had been pushed out of the way, and grass patches were put in a pile. The soil itself looked loose, like it had been moved recently. Fear shot through Linda like a bullet, and she ran to the spot. She started to frantically dig at the dirt while tears were streaming down her face.

"No! No, no, no, no, no," she mumbled and kept digging.

Iversen crossed his arms with a smile and enjoyed the show for a bit. Who knew that seeing Linda fight for someone else's life would be just as entertaining as watching the life drain from their eyes?

He walked around her. Linda was still panting frantically, not at all bothered with what he was doing. She was so determined to save Andrea, that she didn't once consider her own life. She was digging, shouting Andrea's name, and completely blocked out everything else.

She was so consumed with saving a life, that she didn't see it coming. She didn't see him pick it up. She didn't see him swing it. She didn't register it till it was too late.

The shovel swung through the air and hit her in the back of her head. She fell to the ground lifeless, and the shovel was tossed to the ground next to her.

CHAPTER 31

Andrea was cursing as she drove down the highway. An accident further up had completely blocked traffic, and it looked like she would be stuck there for hours. She had hurried into work after the call from her colleague, just to find out they had resolved the matter before she even got there, and no one had bothered with calling to inform her.

She had picked up a few things from the office and informed the department that she'd be working from home for a few days, wanting to take care of Linda once she got discharged from the hospital.

Thirty minutes, and the queue of cars had not moved an inch. She had hoped to have been back at the hospital before Linda woke up, but that was definitely not going to happen now. She cursed herself for having left in the first place and hoped Linda would be okay with waking up on her own.

A lot had happened last night, and they had a lot to talk about. Andrea just hoped that Linda wouldn't take it the wrong way that she had left. *Maybe I should have left her a note?* she thought. *I should have left her a note; why didn't I do that?*

She tried to relax back into the seat and switched on the radio, had her own little highway party as sang along and tried to pass time. Beyonce was playing, and soon the volume was so high, Andrea could no longer hear her own voice. She was moving and grooving in the seat, completely consumed by the music, not hearing her mobile ringing from her purse on the back seat.

It looked like the accident was clearing up now, so it wouldn't be long before she was on her way.

Her mobile rang again. The song had ended, so she heard it and fumbled for her purse behind her seat, but the strap got caught on something, and the content of her purse ended up spilling onto the seat and the bottom of the car. She watched as her phone slid from the purse and did a roll on the seat before falling to the floor, and it stopped ringing.

Another Beyonce song came on, and she decided to leave the phone. Her priority was getting out of traffic and then reaching the hospital. A missed phone call was the last thing on her mind right now; it was probably just someone from work calling, anyway.

Her phone rang again after she parked the car at the hospital. She had been stuck in traffic for an hour and a half. Stretching her legs felt like the biggest release, and there was a big smile on her face as she answered the phone.

"Miss Williams speaking. Oh, hi, Arnold. What can I do for you?" She walked through the front doors of the hospital. "Yes, I literally just walked through the doors. I had to step out for work and then I got stuck in traffic. No, I haven't seen her since this morning, but hold up, let me check my phone." The smile from before had turned to a frown. "I have two missed calls from her, but why are you asking? She is right upstairs; I can just get her to call you when I see her." She listened for a minute and then replied, "What do you mean, she is not here? Of course, she is here. I just saw her this morning." The call ended, and she saw Arnold hurry up the stairs behind her. "What is going on?"

"I am sorry, but she is not here," Arnold said.

Andrea scoffed and walked to her room, expecting to find Linda in the bed. The room was empty, and all her clothes were gone. On the bed was her phone and some paper.

"Where is she?" Arnold looked down and picked up the letter.

"If she had to meet up with the Angel Maker, do you have any idea where they would go?"

"Meet up with him?" Andrea screeched and grabbed the letter from his hands. "Oh, no. No Linda, no, no, no! What have you done? What has she done?" she asked and looked at Arnold. The worried look in his eyes made her anxious, and she grabbed the collar of his shirt roughly and snapped, "Where is she?"

"Andrea—"

"No, don't 'Andrea' me. Where is she, Arnold? How did she even get out of here? Weren't there officers outside her room all night?"

"We are not sure how, but we have looked all over the hospital, and she is not here."

"I can see that," Andrea screamed back and sat down on the bed. "We have to find her," she continued in a calmer tone.

"We will, Andrea. We will find her, I promise you."

Iversen showed his ID and pulled into the building. The whole place was still under lockdown, but of course he had access as one of the leading investigators on the case. It was risky going here. The police, his colleagues, were right outside, but it was also exciting. Like having sex in a public place, the thrill of maybe getting caught, and the sweet victory of getting away with it.

He opened the trunk of his car and looked at the lifeless body before him.

"I am sorry, my angel, but there is no other way. This is the only way we can be together. This way, we will be together forever." He lifted her out of the trunk.

He walked her down to the basement, where she had been held captive all those years ago, and laid her on the concrete. He removed the hair from her face and studied her for a minute.

"Beautiful," he whispered, stroking her cheek. "Angel perfection."

His hand moved lower and unbuttoned her shirt. He pulled her arm from the sleeve and continued to undress her upper half till she was just wearing a sports bra. The excitement made his hands shake. He had to calm his breath a little before slowly turning her around and placing her face down on the concrete. A small gasp went through him as he laid his eyes upon her back. "A masterpiece." He almost couldn't get the words out, his voice trembling and his hands shaking as he made contact with her skin.

Her wings were even more perfect now. The scar tissue had had created a weblike connection between the lines. It wasn't symmetrical, but it was like an imperfect perfection. A tear rolled over his cheek, and he had to remind himself to keep breathing.

He undid his own shirt and looked at his own back in the broken mirror. "Now we both have wings. My angel and I, joined together in heaven forever." He undid his jeans and let go of his arousal, one last time.

His dream was finally coming true. He waited so long. Years went by, and the fantasy just grew greater. Now it was finally time. "I told you, I would come find you." He smiled and tied her hands and feet.

Now that they were together, he had to hurry. Couldn't risk anyone interrupting them, or for his angel to wake up. He swallowed the pills he had with him and laid down beside her. "Here we come," he said and waited for the cigarette he had placed upstairs to burn down and ignite the firetrap he had prepared.

Burning away the past and sending them on their way to the future. To paradise, where all his angels would be waiting for him and his queen.

CHAPTER 32

Linda stirred with a pounding headache and found herself instinctively reaching for the back of her head, only to find her hands tied to her feet, where all blood circulation felt cut off. She made fists with her hands, trying to get her fingers moving. Her whole body was stiff from cold and exhaustion. She trembled at the feeling of the cold concrete seeping into her bare shoulder as she tried to free herself.

The knots were not tied well, and she figured they had only meant to hold an unconscious person. After a few hard pulls on the rope, she could feel it loosen. She kept pulling and pulling, screamed and kicked with her feet as she pulled upwards with her hands. The rope gave in, and she was free.

Her hands trembled as she rubbed her wrists and tried to get warmth into her stiff fingers. Her head was still spinning, and she carefully felt the back of her head. Pain shot through her, and she almost passed out. Her hand was bloody, and she knew she needed a hospital.

She stayed still for a minute, trying to catch her breath, her lungs not finding any oxygen. That was when she registered the smoke gathering under the ceiling. Thick black smoke. She coughed again and looked around. Iversen was lying next to her, seemingly unconscious.

"Iversen," she called and found her voice hoarse and thick. "Iversen," she cried louder and heard the sound of glass exploding somewhere. A shiver ran down her spine at the thought. She could feel the concrete getting warmer. *I am going to burn alive.* Realisation hit her as the flames crept closer.

She was going to die.

The thought shouldn't scare her. It didn't scare her. Dying wasn't scary, and just the other day, she had tried taking her own life. No, dying wasn't scary, yet quivers ran down her spine, and she felt her heart pick up speed. Why did she piss herself from the sheer thought of dying?

She knew why. It was not dying that scared her. At this point, death seemed like a relief, a mercy she had earned through the years. No, it wasn't dying that made her urinate herself. It wasn't the thought of death that had her trembling, moving frantically to try and wake Iversen and get out. No, it wasn't dying. It was the flames. The fire, the burning alive bit that made her act irrationally.

"Come on, you bastard," she cursed as she picked him up over her shoulders and stumbled through the door towards the stairs. The fire was even worse here. Felt like her skin was melting off just by being near it.

She fought her way up the stairs as a beam fell and blocked the main exit. The ground floor was all in flames. She couldn't see anywhere out. Her lungs filled with smoke and felt like they were on fire. "Come on, Hemmer, come on," she shouted, as she coughed and found a free passage to the stairs leading upward.

She stumbled on a step and sprained her ankle as she tried not to drop Iversen.

I should leave him, right? Everyone would understand if I left him behind.

She lowered him from her shoulders and instinctively reached for her ankle. The heat from the fire was hurting her eyes, and her lungs were fighting for every breath. She took of her trousers and tied them around her face, screaming as the knot touched her open wound. An overwhelming feeling of nausea overtook her, and she had to take a second to steady her stomach before continuing.

She felt for a pulse in Iversen, slightly praying there wasn't one so she wouldn't feel bad for leaving him.

"Shit," she mumbled. He was alive. Leaving him here now would be murder. She sighed, pushed the pain aside, picked him up again, and continued up the stairs.

The first floor was just as bad, and the flames had grown in intensity. She figured it wouldn't be long before the whole place exploded. She had trouble seeing anything, and her breaths were so short and raspy now that it felt like no oxygen was left.

This is it. This is how I die, she thought as she went up the last staircase to the second floor. The flames were dominating here as well, but a few of the windows were still free. That's when she made a decision: She would rather fall to her death than be burned alive.

"Come on, Iversen, we are getting out of here." She put him down by the window and started smashing it with a stool she found nearby. People on the street were gasping and pointing towards her. The firefighters yelled something her way, but she couldn't hear anything for the flames.

She picked up Iversen and aimed for the sheet that it looked like the firefighters were holding. She watched as his body fell towards the ground and landed in the sheet, and she praised herself lucky that they were only on the second floor. They could make it; according to science, they could make it.

Her turn. She closed her eyes and thought of all the times she and Tucker had practiced a jump like this. "Jump and roll; jump and roll," she repeated to herself as the firefighters got the sheet ready again.

All angels have wings, she thought. Bent her knees, ready to jump.

The oxygen from the now open window had fuelled the fire, and before she could jump, the second floor exploded, and her body was blown out the window. The blast knocked her unconscious before she even started falling.

Arnold had tried to call Iversen, needing him out there looking for Linda. The lack of response from his colleague angered him. He almost flipped the desk over. He felt a pain in his chest and sat down. He closed his eyes and forced his breath to even out. He grabbed a pill from his prescription box and swallowed it, grabbed the glass of water on his desk to help guide it down. A couple of deep breaths later, and he felt the pain subside. With the pain going went the anger too, and he was able to focus.

He picked up the folder in front of him and went through the materials again. There had to be a hint in here somewhere as to where this special meeting spot would be. He knew Linda had only seen the house during her captivity, and part of him thought that had to be the place, but it couldn't be that simple. He could not let go of the nagging feeling that the house was involved somehow, and he sent a patrol car to the location. They were to prevent any unauthorised activity and report to him.

That cleared some of his worry and freed up some space in his mind to think.

"Where did you go? What place is special to you?" he mumbled to himself as he paced around the room. His eyes fell on the whiteboard with pictures of all the murdered women. "You didn't take trophies. Why didn't you?" He walked closer to the board and scanned it again. "The stones, you placed small tombstones on the graves, why? Did you take pictures of them? Did you like knowing that the graves were visible yet hidden, like a secret? Your secret." He stood unmoving for a bit and went over it all again. "This place is special to you, isn't it, the forest? This is your space, your secret."

Inspiration hit him. He grabbed his phone and almost ran towards the exit while gathering people for backup. He tried dialling Iversen again while in the car, but no luck. "Damn it, Iversen, answer your phone," he yelled as a voicemail and tossed the phone onto the passenger seat. He flipped on the siren and floored the accelerator.

It was obvious that someone had been there. A trail of blood was visible in the snow, and fresh tire marks showed in the parking lot. *It's too late. I got here too late*, Arnold thought and cursed himself. "Seal off the area. No one in or out if they are not in uniform, got it?"

His phone started ringing, and he answered it a bit more aggressively than intended. "Yes, what is it, Holland? Who? Iversen? What is he doing at the house? Well, why didn't you ask him? Never mind, I am going there myself."

Annoyed, he got back in his car and tried calling Iversen again, definitely demanding an explanation once he found that young man.

CHAPTER 33

Arnold barely made it into town before his phone was ringing again. "Yes, Holland, what now?" The officer on the phone was stuttering and out of breath. "Fire? What do you mean, the place is on fire? I thought you were watching it?" Arnold felt a knot in his stomach. "Is Iversen still in there? Shit, wait for the fire department; I'll be there in five." He hung up and sped faster.

Fire trucks and ambulances were already on site by the time Arnold arrived. They had done a sweep of all three floors and not found anyone, thought they did see Iversen's car in the garage and had pulled it out for evidence, as there was blood all over the trunk.

"Let me see it," Arnold said and was taken to the car. All colour drained from his face at the realisation. "And you have checked all floors?"

"Yes, sir."

"Including the basement?" Arnold asked, knowing that the basement door to the property was hidden. The whole purpose of this place had been to keep the basement hidden. Hide fugitives or kidnap little girls.

"There is no basement, sir," the firefighter said, and Arnold swallowed hard.

"Yes, there is. I have seen it myself. You have to go back in there."

"We cannot go back in, sir; the place is too unstable."

"But we have people down there. I am pretty certain Iversen is down there along with a victim, Linda."

He kept fighting to get inside, but in that moment, the ground floor windows exploded, and the fire spread further. *No,* his inner thoughts screamed, while he could do nothing but stare, as the flames spread to the first and second floor. Soon the whole building looked like one flame.

"Arnold? Arnold?" a female voice called from somewhere behind him. Annelise and Andrea walked towards him and panicked at the sight of the fire.

"Is she in there, Arnold? Is she in there?" Andrea asked but never got an answer.

Arnold just lowered his eyes as tears started to fall. The scream that erupted from Andrea sent a shock through them all. Everyone on the street felt the tears press on, as they listened to the flames and the woman's agonising cries. No one said anything. They all just looked to the house and prayed for the souls lost in the fire.

Annelise wrapped Andrea in her arms while she fought her own tears.

"It was Iversen," Arnold said quietly and met his wife's eyes. "The Angel Maker; it's Iversen."

"Impossible," she whispered, but could see in her husband's eyes that it was true. Nausea rolled through her, as she remembered all the times Iversen had spent at their house. All the times he had played with her grandchildren and shared a hug with them. "Iversen," she whispered and felt Andrea tense in her arms.

"Linda told me he was aggressive towards her once," Andrea said. "He had shared his feelings for her, and she had not reciprocated, and he had gotten angry. Aggressive. She had kicked him out, and it had sent her into a panic attack." Andrea felt her fists tighten at the thought.

"Now that you mention it," Arnold said, "I think I went there that day. Took me a long time to calm her down."

How had he not seen it? Had Iversen really been that good an actor? Had there been no signs? He kept cracking his brain to find answers. Part of him wanted to find another explanation as to why Iversen's car was filled with blood, and why his car was here at the house, what he was doing here in the first place. Any other explanation than him being the Angel Maker. Any other. He just couldn't find any. Nothing else made sense. Iversen had to be the one. He had to be the killer they had been hunting for months now.

Arnold swallowed hard at the thought of all the people his partner had murdered. The latest, the woman and her child, he had raped repeatedly. Arnold felt sick. This time, he could not hold it in. He turned and emptied his stomach contents onto the pavement.

Annelise went to check on him, when suddenly people started shouting and pointing to the building. A window on the second floor was shattered, and a figure could be seen inside. "Linda," Arnold shouted, and Andrea snapped her head up.

"Linda," they all shouted; they yelled for her to stop, when it looked like she was going to jump.

The firefighters scrambled about and quickly gathered on the street below the house with what looked like a sheet in case she fell down.

"Oh, my God," Arnold said and looked with wide eyes towards Linda, as she was lifting Iversen out the window. "She saved him," he whispered and saw Iversen's body fall from the window. He was caught safely, and Linda seemed to get herself ready.

The fire seemed to inhale, and the fire chief told everyone to get down. The house was going to explode any second, and Linda was still in the window. "Jump," Arnold shouted and waved at Linda to get her attention. "Jump now," he yelled again, as he was tackled by a firefighter, and the blast swallowed his words.

Linda was blown from her spot in the window, and Arnold didn't get to see if they caught her or not.

Andrea froze on the pavement, her eyes catching a glimpse of Linda's in the street.

"Linda." The name came over her lips like a whisper. Her body was covered up and moved to a gurney before she could get a proper look. "Linda," she whispered again and started fighting her way through the crowd. "Linda," she was screaming now, pushing her way to the front, only to be stopped by some officers trying to calm her down. "No, you don't understand; that is my wife," she yelled and started kicking to get loose.

Her heart swelled in her chest till it felt too large for her body. All these years of trying to get over her, and with just one look, one touch, she was back to square one, loving every part of this complex woman. She collapsed in the arms of the officer, wrapped her arms around herself, and screamed, as Annelise and Arnold came to her aid.

"Come on, Holland here will take you and Annelise to the hospital," Arnold said, holding her face in his hands to make sure she was listening. Andrea nodded and followed the officer to the car. Annelise shared a look with her husband before joining Andrea, and the car drove off.

Linda's ambulance was already gone by the time Arnold turned around. He instructed another patrol car to follow Iversen and not leave him out of sight.

"Buch," a voice cut through. Arnold turned to see his friend making his way through the crowd.

"Jensen," Arnold greeted him and surprised him and himself by embracing his longtime friend in a hug. Jensen didn't say anything; he just hugged his friend back and led him to the car so they could talk.

"I didn't get a lot of details from the others, but I understand that Iversen and Hemmer were in the building at the time of the fire?" Jensen asked.

Arnold nodded and began driving towards the hospital.

"Yes. I don't know anything definitively yet, but it seems that Iversen is our Angel Maker." Arnold accelerated, finally getting out of the dense traffic.

Jensen hummed in acknowledgement and then still in his movements.

"Sorry, did I hear you right. Iversen? As in *our* Iversen? He is the Angel Maker?"

"Yes."

"What makes you think that?"

"I don't think it; I know it," Arnold answered and pulled up in front of the hospital. "We need to put a forensics team on his car. The boot is filled with blood, and I suspect it is Linda's. It will most likely be a match to the blood found in the forest at the gravesites."

"I see, but there could be many explanations as to why there is blood in his car and why he is here. Maybe he went here to save Linda. I mean, why else would she save him?"

"That is just who Linda is. She would save even the worst of people." Arnold locked the car. "Look, Jensen, I trust you. Do what you find necessary; just don't let Iversen out of your sight till you know the truth. I am telling you: He is our killer. I can feel it in my gut. It is the only thing making sense anymore. Now, if you will excuse me, I need to go find my friend and call her family."

The hospital smelled like death. Not in the rotting and decay kind of way, but like sadness and latex. Stale and dry. The walls were too white and the lights too bright. Every hallway looked the same: long and never-ending. The combination made Andrea feel nauseous, and even though she'd only been there for a matter of minutes, she suddenly wished she could step outside. Felt the sudden urge to light a cigarette.

The air felt sick, contained. Her hands felt like they were carrying germs. Sticky and clammy, even though she had not physically touched anything aside from the single button in the elevator. She kept fidgeting and felt herself getting more and more impatient as the elevator moved.

Annelise grabbed one of her hands and held it tight. She too was feeling off, had a sick feeling in her stomach. This wasn't fair. Linda didn't deserve this. She was such a good person; why did this keep happening to her?

The resounding clicks of their heels echoed loudly throughout the mostly empty hallway. Occasionally, they would pass a picture frame hung neatly on the wall. Fields of bright yellow flowers, forests of lush and beautiful trees, warm sunsets bursting with hues of reds and yellows and pinks. The pictures looked out of place. Forced, like they didn't belong there. They were actual photographs but they looked fake, unnatural. Andrea studied one as she passed it. It made her feel uncomfortable. Like this place was trying too hard to. But no painting could cover for the anguished feeling it was to walk through the hallways of a hospital, knowing your loved one was somewhere fighting for their life.

She pulled her shawl more tightly around her shoulders. It was not particularly cold, but the slight weight of it felt comforting, familiar, and she clung to it as if it was the only thing keeping her grounded in this moment.

They sat down in the nearby waiting room. Annelise went to get them coffee, and soon after Arnold joined them. He was on the phone with Linda's parents. He was explaining the situation, and Andrea could hear the excruciating cries on the other end. Linda's mother was broken. Her youngest daughter was in the hospital again, and this time, there was no telling if she would make it out alive. After Trish, she couldn't lose another one; she couldn't.

Arnold ended the call and made another one, this time to Linda's brother. After him, her sister and then her brother-in-law.

Soon the waiting room was filled with family, worried faces all praying for Linda and wishing for the best.

The scent of fresh flowers was everywhere. Everyone had brought something but had nowhere to put it. No room to be in, no space to hunker down. Linda was still in surgery, so no room had been assigned to her yet. No news was shared with the family yet. Nothing was known. Nothing but the fact that she had jumped from a burning building and was rushed off in an ambulance.

Darren went to draw the curtains and open the window, allowing the fresh air to flow through the waiting room. The curtains moved gently in the breeze; Andrea shivered and pulled the shawl tighter around her, almost merging it with her body.

"I figured we could use some fresh air," Darren said and sat back down with his two sons.

Andrea's eyes caught the sunlight as it danced across the floor, stretching into the room. Her eyes followed the light to the door, where a set of feet came into her vision.

"Family of Miss Hemmer?" a voice spoke, and everyone stood up at once. Linda's mother walked towards the doctor with careful steps and reached to shake his hand.

"I am her mother," she said.

"Hello, I am Dr. Ovington."

He kept speaking, but Andrea couldn't hear him. She was too focused on everyone's reactions, hoping their faces would tell her if Linda was okay or not. *She is okay, right?* She felt her heart hammer in her chest. She was sure the outline of her heart was visible on her skin, felt like one of those cartoon characters with their hearts beating outside their body. She held her breath, too scared to let oxygen in, too paralysed to even move.

It was just a few days ago that Linda had landed in the hospital last, and though they had all worried, they had known she was okay. This time, they didn't know. This time, her life was literally in the hands of doctors. She remembered the last time she had been in a situation like this, anxiously waiting for good news, any news, just any update to calm this beating heart of hers.

It had been just a regular day. They had been at the park for a picnic. Willa had seen a dog and went to pet it. She had been no more than twenty metres away, and they had had their eyes on her the whole time. It was to this day still the most horrific thing Andrea had ever gone through. The dog had taken off out of the blue, the owner shouting and Willa running after it. Linda had been up in a flash, chasing after their daughter, yelling at her not to run into the street. Andrea had gotten up too, just in time to see the collision.

Linda had been an arm's reach away from Willa when the car had hit. Willa's tiny body had been crushed under the impact, and Linda had broken her arm.

Waiting for the doctors back then had been just as excruciating as now. Only then, she had had Linda by her side. Linda had been her rock and supported her in every way. Now she was alone. Alone, waiting to hear if the love of her life had made it or not.

There was no change in their faces, nothing to read.

The doctor was walking away, but no one seemed to react.

"What is happening?" Andrea asked, and Linda's mother turned to embrace her in a hug.

"She is in a coma," she whispered into Andrea's shoulder.

"In a coma? What does that mean?" Andrea asked but didn't get an answer as she was led by the hand towards Linda's room.

"Come, my dear, let's go see her."

See her, Andrea thought and wasn't sure if she wanted to.

The first thing she noticed was the light dancing across the floor again. It stretched into the room, and small beams of it landed on the immovable body in the bed.

Andrea swallowed hard at the sight of Linda's bracelet on the bedside table. Willa had made that bracelet for her, and Linda had never taken it off.

Until now, part of her had been able to tell herself that it was someone else she was visiting, someone she didn't care for as much as her Linda, but seeing that bracelet made it all too real, and that was before she even let her eyes fall on Linda's shape.

She walked towards the bed and gently reached forward to take her ex-wife's hand in her own. There was no response, no sign that Linda had any idea she was even there. Not a single twitch. She swallowed and allowed her eyes to roam over the body, examining the damage that had been caused.

The cut at the back of Linda's head had been stitched together, and she had bandages all around her head. Some of her hair had burned off, and Andrea guessed there were severe burn marks all over her body, given the amount of bandages wrapped around her arms. Her left eye was purple and swollen, and the breathing tube covered most of her face, making her almost unrecognisable.

It all seemed so bizarre. Unreal.

The woman before her didn't look like Linda. Her eyes were sunken, her cheeks were pale, and her body looked rigid. Wires and tubes sprouted from every direction and connected to machines that beeped and clacked loudly with a constant stream of blinking lights. Her skin was void of all colours, and the white hospital gown made her skin look harsh and cold. It was all wrong. Linda was warm and gentle. This wasn't Linda; this was just an empty shell that barely resembled her.

Footsteps approached from behind, and a figure hovered in the doorway.

"Andrea." The sound of her voice made her release a breath she didn't realise she was holding. "She is strong. She will be okay."

Andrea felt a hand on her shoulder, and that was all it took for her to break. She cried and almost lost her balance before she felt a pair of strong arms wrap around her and hold her tight. "I am glad you are here," Arnold said. "There is no one Linda would rather see than you."

CHAPTER 34

Summer was in full bloom, the sun filling the streets with high temperatures and not a cloud in the sky. The city filled with sunburned tourists and happy couples. Kids were playing in the fountain or standing in line for ice cream.

Andrea watched from her apartment as everyone laughed and enjoyed the summer just outside her window. She scoffed as an elderly couple started dancing to the local street artist playing a few feet away. She drank until the scotch no longer burned on its way down, until she felt numb to the agony that had made her reach for the bottle in the first place. She stumbled as she stood up from her seat at the window, stubbed her toe on the coffee table as she place the bottle to go curl up in bed, but she didn't care. She barely felt it.

She sighed, a sigh that felt heavier than the burden she was carrying.

The apartment was a mess. A real mess, spectacular achievement for someone who was rarely home, though all she had done lately was stay at home. She looked around, figured cleaning was better left for some other day. Today was for piecing herself back together and preparing to do the same again tomorrow.

She stripped off her dress and let it fall to the floor, left it there as she walked towards the bedroom. She caught a sight of herself in the mirror and sucked in a breath, as she studied herself. Her hands shook as they pushed her hair to the side away from her face, horrified at the person staring back at her. The mirror was not her friend. It hung there on the wall, judging every flaw and screaming for her to put her clothes back on. Maybe it was right; maybe she should stay covered. Linda would have told the mirror to go fuck itself; she would probably even have put up a fight with it if she had seen the state it had left Andrea in. The thought made

Andrea smile a little. Tears stinging the corners of her eyes and disgust clawing at her chest at the sight of herself.

She sighed, turned away from the mirror, and curled up in the bed, buried in the sheets that she had yet to replace. *Later*, she thought. *Later*.

She closed her eyes and disappeared into her memories. The place where she could feel safe and where Linda was still Linda.

> She had been out for drinks with her friend Samuel. They had just discussed moving onto the next spot when three women walked in. They were sisters, that much was clear. Each looking like the other and yet looking so much different. Andrea had immediately recognised the taller one; she was the one from the elevator just a few days ago. What was her name again?
>
> She didn't get far in her thoughts, as Samuel was waving them over, and the tall one took a seat next to Andrea.
>
> "Hi, again." She smiled, and Andrea had lost all cognitive function. Samuel had given her a kick under the table, and she had finally taken the woman's hand and introduced herself. "You do remember me, right? My name is Linda; we met in the elevator the other day."
>
> *Linda*, Andrea thought to herself and again found herself lost in the bright-blue eyes.
>
> "Are you a witch?" The words were out of her mouth before she could stop them, and the whole table cracked up laughing, but it seemed to have broken the awkwardness.
>
> "No." Linda laughed. "I am no witch. Though I have been told that I am an angel."
>
> Andrea just smiled and figured that if angels were real, then Linda was definitely one of them.
>
> The night had gone by quickly. Andrea and Linda had talked the whole time, never once looked away from each other. Samuel had just rolled his eyes at his friend and enjoyed seeing her make a fool of herself.

At the end of the night, Linda and her sisters said their goodbyes, and Andrea was stuck in a trance, watching as Linda exited the bar.

"Hello. Earth to Andy."

"What?"

Samuel rolled his eyes again and made a comment about her being a useless-gay.

"Hey, I am not," she defended herself and crossed her arms over her chest.

"Really? She asked you out, but you were too busy staring at her ass to notice."

"I- I- I have no defence against that," she mumbled as she gazed towards the door.

"Exactly; the prosecution rests."

"I hate you," Andrea whispered and collected her coat.

"Well, she definitely wanted to get in your pants." Samuel would not drop the subject, and Andrea felt a blush creep on her face.

"No, she does not seem like the type," Andrea said, but didn't quite believe it herself.

"Hate to be the one to break this to you, love, but you are hot. Everyone's the type to bang you," Samuel explained, and Andrea just scoffed.

"Sure, Sam," she laughed and got in the Uber. Yet she couldn't help but smile at the thought that Linda might have wanted her.

She was smiling in her sleep, dreaming of how she and Linda first got together, and how their relationship had been jump-started after that night in the bar.

A loud banging sounded on the door and distracted her from her sleep. Reluctantly, she got out of bed and made her way towards the door. Annelise and Arnold stood on the outside and looked shocked to see her in this state.

"Andrea," Annelise exclaimed and quickly moved to cover her up. "Go get dressed, honey," she said and pushed her towards the bedroom. A quick glance around the apartment didn't get her any less concerned. She shared a look with her husband and followed Andrea into the bedroom.

Arnold sighed heavily and felt his nostrils tickle. This space hadn't seen fresh air in weeks, maybe even months. He opened a few windows and started collecting all leftover takeout in large bags. Once he was done with that, he could hear the shower running. How Annelise had managed to get Andrea in there was beyond him. It was clear from it all that she was done with life. She wasn't living anymore; she was barely existing.

The garbage bags were placed by the door. He would have his son come pick them up later.

His eyes fell on a photo on a shelf by the door. It was of Andrea, Linda, and Willa in a human pyramid. He smiled briefly; what a lovely family they had been. His eyes grew sad again and took it out on the dishes. Started scrubbing them clean before putting them in the dishwasher.

The shower switched off again, and he could hear some muffled voices coming from the bedroom. Not long after, Andrea stepped out, all dressed and looking presentable.

"Let's have a cup of coffee before we leave," Annelise suggested and put a pot on while Arnold cleaned some mugs and sat down next to Andrea.

"I am not going to ask how you are doing; I think that's pretty obvious at this point, but I hope you know we are here whenever you need us." Arnold gently took Andrea's hand in his.

Andrea nodded slowly. The shower having washed away months of filth and self-loath. Now that she was feeling human again, her vulnerability came crashing down, and she started sobbing uncontrollably. Neither Arnold nor Annelise said anything; they just sat with her, drank their coffee, and waited for the sobbing to subside.

Once Andrea was ready, they went out to the car and drove out of town to a clinic not far from there.

"Wait," Andrea whispered, as they made their way towards the entrance.

"We are here with you, honey," Annelise said, grabbing her hand. "We are all here together."

"You have been here before, right?" Andrea asked, and the couple nodded. "How is she?"

"She is alive, dear. That is all that matters."

Andrea nodded and followed them inside. They were led down a hallway to a big common room. Lots of people were occupying the space, each at their own table with loved ones. Some were drinking coffee and sharing a cake, while others were playing a game or simply just talking.

"Here we are, dear," Annelise said; Andrea followed her gaze and instantly recognised the woman in front of them.

"Linda!" She sobbed and took a few breaths to steady herself before sitting down across from her. The sight was like a sucker punch to her stomach. If she thought the view of herself in the mirror was shocking, it was nothing compared to seeing her ex-wife. Linda's face was frail and her eyes blank. Her arms were covered in scar tissue from burns and skin grafts, and her whole posture crumbled forward like an old man.

"Linda?" Andrea spoke again and looked at Annelise, when there was no response.

"Go on, dear, talk. We will be right over here." Annelise smiled.

Andrea looked back at her ex-wife, her eyes filling with tears. She sniffled and picked at the table edge, trying to come up with something to say. Then she felt a hand in hers, and a gasp went through the nurse at her side.

"She has never done that before. We have not had any reaction in the past six months, let alone one this significant," the nurse explained.

Andrea swallowed and took a chance, squeezing the hand a little. The tiniest of a squeeze was returned. Now tears were freefalling, and Andrea didn't care that she looked like an idiot. Linda was alive, and there was now hope that she could come back.

Lightning Source UK Ltd.
Milton Keynes UK
UKHW012116231122
412695UK00001B/7